"In Vino Veritas"

*"Or whatever the hell the word is for beer,"
Larry said with a laugh. "Lila's the world's
slickest liar. Don't you know that, Nancy?
It took me quite a while to get on to it.
What's more, she's a psychopathic liar. She
actually prefers lying to telling the truth.
She has no conscience, no sense of the difference between right and wrong. She's sick
in the head, and there's no cure for it except
to put her out of her misery, the way you'd
shoot a rabid dog."*

If Larry Connor had *sounded* drunk, Nancy
would simply have jumped up from the
bench and gone away. But he did not sound
drunk. On the contrary, he sounded cold
stone sober, even deliberate. . . .

Other SIGNET Ellery Queen Titles

THE NEW AMERICAN LIBRARY, INC.,
P.O. Box 999, Bergenfield, New Jersey 07621

Blow Hot, Blow Cold

by
ELLERY QUEEN

A SIGNET BOOK
NEW AMERICAN LIBRARY
TIMES MIRROR

SIGNET TRADEMARK REG. U.S. PAT. OFF. AND FOREIGN COUNTRIES
REGISTERED TRADEMARK—MARCA REGISTRADA
HECHO EN CHICAGO, U.S.A.

SIGNET, SIGNET CLASSICS, MENTOR, PLUME AND MERIDIAN BOOKS
are published by The New American Library, Inc.,
1301 Avenue of the Americas, New York, New York 10019

FIRST PRINTING, AUGUST, 1974

1 2 3 4 5 6 7 8 9

PRINTED IN THE UNITED STATES OF AMERICA

The story is that a man, eating with a Satyr one winter day, blew on his hands, and when the Satyr asked him why, he answered that it was to warm his hands. Then when he found the soup too hot, he blew on it. The Satyr asked again why he did so, and the man replied that it was to cool the soup. "Then," said the Satyr, "I renounce your friendship, because you blow hot and cold out of the same mouth."

—AESOP, *Fables (c. 570 B.C.)*

Cast of Characters

1

From where she sat at her kitchen table in Shady Acres Addition, Nancy Howell could see through the open window and across the low hedge into the backyard of th next-door house, owned and occupied by Larry and Lila Connor. The Connors had a flagstone terrace behind their house, and Nancy kept waiting and watching for Lila Connor to come out in her modified bikini and start sunning herself on the terrace. This afternoon Lila hadn't come out so far, and it didn't look as if she was going to. The reason was probably that it was just too hot. It was over a hundred degrees in the sun, and you had to be pretty careful about getting burned even if you were already toasty brown all over, as Nancy and Lila both were.

What Nancy had in mind to do if Lila appeared was to get into a modified bikini of her own and go over to join Lila on the Connor terrace. Not that Nancy really wanted to lie in the sun on this particular afternoon. What she had in mind was to get herself invited into Lila's house. It was much too hot to lie in the sun for more than fifteen minutes or so; Lila would surely go inside again, and she would just as surely invite Nancy to go with her.

The point was, Lila's house was air-conditioned and Nancy's was not. Well, that wasn't quite true; actually, the upstairs bedroom that Nancy shared with David had a window unit. But that wasn't the same as central air-conditioning, with breezes flowing deliciously through all the furnace ducts and pouring through the vents into every room. It gave you a kind of exciting—really sensual—feeling (especially if all you had on was a bikini) to move from room to room in all that wonderful coolness. It seemed like such a waste for Lila to be over there alone while Nancy steamed under the hot breath of a mere window fan and perspiration seeped from her brown skin and trickled between her alert breasts.

Nancy felt a twitch of guilt. Not for envying Lila her air-conditioning, but because the envy implied a criticism of David that she certainly did not intend. David was her pleasure and pride. Nancy understood perfectly well that central air-conditioning could rarely be afforded by schoolteachers, of whom David was one, while by successful accountants, of whom Larry Connors was one, it rarely couldn't, so to speak. Her love and loyalty were fiercely David's, no question about that; but at the same time Nancy was compelled to admit to herself that Larry Connor was a pretty attractive guy, too, and was quite capable of arousing ideas in the head of a girl who might have drunk a couple of Martinis on an empty stomach. Mae Walters, who lived in the split-level across the alley on the other side of the block, didn't like Larry and Lila very much; but Nancy liked them both, and so did David, even though they did not seem to be particularly happy and often said cruel things to each other in front of other people.

Nancy looked at her wrist watch, which David had given her for Christmas three years ago, before they were married. It was exactly three o'clock. You couldn't depend on its being exactly three o'clock just because the watch said so, but you could at least depend on its being somewhere near it; anyhow, it was becoming apparent that Lila wasn't coming out on her terrace to sun herself.

Nancy sighed and gave up hope. What she would do,

she decided, was fix herself a tall, cold gin-and-tonic and go upstairs to the bedroom with the window unit. Maybe she would lie down and take a nap. Then, before she knew it, it would be five o'clock, and David would be home from high school, where he was working all day even though it was Saturday. (David was teaching corrective English in the summer session because they needed the extra money, and this was quite a sacrifice for him to make, because according to David nobody took corrective English but blockheads. He was often quite cross when he came home, and it required the most careful application of gin and tenderness in the right proportions to get him in a good humor again.)

Having decided what to do, Nancy rose and automatically tugged at her shorts, which had stuck to her thighs. She dropped ice cubes into a tall glass and filled the glass with gin and quinine water. Then she went out into the little hall and upstairs to the bedroom.

It was cool in the room, a sharp change from the rest of the house, and she became aware really for the first time how clammy her blouse and shorts were. She would simply have to take a shower; so she set the glass on a table beside the bed, got out of her shorts and blouse, and pattered to the bathroom. She lingered under a warm shower, then took a quick cold one, wriggling with pleasure under the needle-spray.

Back in the bedroom, Nancy inspected herself in the full-length mirror on the back of the closet door. She was pleased with what she saw. It was certainly not inferior to anything Lila Connor would have seen in the same circumstances . . . She thought, smiling, that the two lighter bands above and below looked positively obscene. It was a shame that there was nowhere to lie naked in the sun in privacy. It was a necessary concession to neighborhood opinion even to wear modified bikinis instead of extreme ones. Mae Walters, for example, did not approve of bikinis at all, especially when her Stanley was around; Mae had said more than once in the hearing of Nancy and Lila that she considered a clear white skin to be "much more attractive" than skin burned by the sun. Moreover, according to Mae, the sun dried out the natural oils and caused premature wrinkles. Nancy smiled again at her unwrinkled image.

Feeling cool and clean, she went over to the bed and sat on the edge and picked up her glass. She drank the gin-and-tonic slowly, thinking with anticipation of the evening ahead. Jack and Vera Richmond were having a backyard barbecue, to which the Howells and the Connors and the Walterses were invited, and that meant she would not have to fix dinner in a hot kitchen or painfully weigh assets against expenses with David to see if they could possibly afford dinner out. The Richmonds lived in a stone ranch-style to the other side of the Connors; Jack Richmond was a doctor, which was even more profitable than accountancy. But Jack and Vera were unpretentious and good mixers, at ease with everyone. They were perhaps ten years older than the Howells and the Walterses and the Connors, who had all voted nationally at least once but not more than twice.

The gin-and-tonic had moved by swallows from the tall glass to Nancy's stomach, where it was beginning to glow. She deposited the glass on the bedside table and threw herself down on the bed.

She began to wish that David would come home. But he had said five o'clock, and it was now only about three-thirty. An hour and a half was a long time for a girl to lie on her back wishing for her husband, Nancy thought drowsily, and the next thing she knew her eyes flew open and there he was, on the edge of the bed, contemplating her navel. She sat up and put her arms around his neck and the situation immediately became fraught with possibilities.

"Darling," Nancy breathed in David's ear, "here you are at last."

"Here, as a matter of fact," he said, stroking her back, "we both are."

"Have you had a good day?"

"No. My day has been hellishly hot. Also frustrating."

"How frustrating? You don't have classes on Saturday."

"But I have papers to grade that are the work of classes. It's absolutely fantastic how little can be learned by a conscientious blockhead if he really tries."

"You mustn't expect too much from students who are forced to take corrective English, darling. It isn't reasonable."

"True. Thank God for the curve," David said, tracing one of Nancy's with an absent finger. "It's a wonderful device. By applying it, you can change an F to a C and a C to an A in the wink of an eye."

"David, that *tickles!*" Nancy giggled, slapping his hand.

She leaned shamelessly back against the headboard and observed him with what might have seemed excessive enthusiasm. To be honest, David wasn't exceptional to observe; Nancy's overenthusiasm was the effect of some mysterious affinity she did not understand. She had felt it from the first instant of meeting. She still felt it, and she was ready and willing to feel it forever, even though his short hair was a color you could only call neutral, his hands and feet were a good deal larger than the rest of him called for, and his nose was almost as crooked as his smile. David was nothing, in short, that should be considered a threat to a girl's chemistry or modesty; but here was hers in pleasant peril nonetheless. It was altogether a satisfactory state of affairs.

"Darling," Nancy murmured, her eyes half-closed, "what time is it?"

"Five-thirty. Why?" asked David, reaching.

Nancy rolled swiftly over out of range.

"I am merely budgeting what is left of the day. At seven we're expected in the Richmonds' backyard for the barbecue. Meanwhile a great *deal* can be accomplished. Would you like to take a shower to begin with?"

"I'd rather not," said David hungrily, "but I guess I'd better."

"As a favor to me, darling, make it . . . quick?"

So David leaped for the bathroom, and Nancy waited until she heard the shower. Then she slipped off the bed and over to her dressing table and drew a brush through her fair short hair three or four times with an air of abstraction. Afterward she peered through the curtains at an angle up the macadam street. At the curb in front of the Richmonds' stood the delivery truck of the local beer distributor. The driver was pushing a small hand-truck up the Richmond walk bearing a metal keg of beer with a spigot and pump attachment for drawing the beer under pressure, as at a bar.

Altogether, Nancy thought, what with David here and the keg there, the day was looking up. Then she had no time to think of anything but the immediate present, for David was coming at her, still toweling himself, with a leer of purest lust.

"Defend yourself, baby!"

"Who needs it?" murmured Nancy, opening her arms.

2

The party, as it turned out, wasn't a barbecue after all. No deception was intended, of course; it had merely become a tribal tradition to refer to backyard cookouts as barbecues. It was actually a hamburger fry, or broil, or whatever—they were cooked by Jack Richmond on a grill over charcoal. Dr. Jack Richmond was positively paranoid about his ability to cook hamburgers just right on a charcoal grill, and it was *verboten* to help him or interfere in any way. The fact that he wore a starched chef's cap and an apron was misleading; his hamburgers were really as good as he claimed.

Nancy in shorts and David in slacks, having accomplished a great deal in the meanwhile, went over at seven. They cut across the Connors' backyard, and while they were on the way a window was opened suddenly and Larry Connor's voice shouted out.

"Hey, you guys! We'll be with you in a few minutes."

Nancy and David waved at the window, which immediately closed, and went on across a second low hedge into the Richmonds' yard and onto the terrace where Dr. Jack was watching a beautiful bed of glowing coals with stern concentration. He turned and raised a coal tongs in salute, and Nancy was forced to admit—to herself—that he was probably the handsomest man she had ever known. She wondered how she could be so objective about it. Maybe it indicated a kind of perversion or

15

something. Was it abnormal to prefer a crooked nose to a beautifully straight one?

"Welcome, neighbors," Jack said. "Wasn't that old Larry bellowing at you?"

"Yes," Nancy said. "He said he and Lila would be here in a few minutes."

"I must say he sounded in good humor. Let's hope it lasts."

"Oh, Larry's all right," David said.

"Sure, and Lila's a great gal, and they're a charming couple. But when they get to cutting each other up, it makes things a little tense."

Nancy had to concede that it did, but she conceded it silently, to herself. She didn't think Jack Richmond ought to talk about Lila and Larry Connor like that, even though it was true. There was certainly a bitterness between them that exploded unexpectedly, especially when they had been drinking. Nancy supposed it was because Lila wasn't particularly choosy in exploiting her sex appeal, which was considerable. Although Larry wasn't exactly inhibited in certain circumstances either, as Nancy could testify from a couple of personal experiences. Anyhow, she didn't think there was any real nymphomania in Lila. In fact, Nancy suspected that Lila was on the chilly side, under that almost feverish exterior; sometimes Lila gave her the impression of a rather cruel duplicity. Take, for example, the way she worked on poor old Stanley Walters. Stanley was no woman's dream, that was for sure, and there was something sickening in the way Lila deliberately excited him so that he lost the use of the few wits he had. In Nancy's opinion, Lila did it to irritate Stanley's wife; it probably didn't occur to Lila how cruel it was to Stanley, who got nothing from Lila and hell from Mae, and so was the victim of both. Nancy shrugged. She liked Lila in spite of everything, and she had no wish to continue the conversation Jack Richmond had begun.

Fortunately, at that moment Vera Richmond came out of the house toting a large wooden bowl full of sliced tomatoes and cucumbers and onions in sweetened vinegar. Vera set the bowl down on a table, and Nancy went over to greet her and see if she could help. Vera said she could.

"Darling," Vera said, "such *beautiful* brown legs. It's bitchy of you to wear shorts and show the rest of us up."

Vera herself was wearing shorts, and the reason she was so generous in the matter of Nancy's legs was that she really had nothing to worry about in the matter of her own. Vera's face was characterized by too much nose and too many teeth; but her legs were long and lovely, and if they were in fact slightly inferior to Nancy's, that was surely nothing to make a federal case about.

Nancy said something appropriate, and Vera laughed, showing her long upper teeth. She took Nancy into the kitchen, where other platters and bowls and trays of goodies were waiting to be brought out. One thing about Vera Richmond, you could always expect the best at her parties. Even at a little do like this, for a few close neighbors, featuring hamburgers. No ground meat that was 50 per cent fat—Vera always bought the most expensive grade of ground top round, and delicious side-things to go with them. She had been a nurse at the hospital where Jack Richmond interned, and she had come from a very poor family whose many children never got enough to eat.

It took two more trips to get everything out to the terrace. By that time Lila and Larry Connor had come over from next door and Mae and Stanley Walters from across the alley. Lila was talking with David, Larry was talking with Mae, and Stanley was standing by the grill with Jack, who had started grilling the big luscious-looking patties of dark red meat that he was taking from a portable ice chest. Everyone was nuzzling a goblet of beer.

"Hey," Nancy said, "how come everybody has a beer except the workers?"

Stanley Walters went over to the keg and drew two beers and presented them to Nancy and Vera with what he pathetically meant to be a gallant flourish. Stanley ran to clumsy fat, and there was a kind of unintentional clownishness about everything he did that was more absurd than comic. He had come to town as manager of a chain shoe store, but he had lost his job and Mae had made him take a big bank loan and go into business for himself. His shop (Shoes For The Family At Family Prices) was finally prospering after a shaky start. The bank loan was almost paid off. Mae kept his books straight, and she kept Stanley straight, too. Mae was tall and had light red hair and white skin that couldn't tolerate the sun. She was not overweight for her height, but she had large breasts and hips that made her seem heavier than she was.

"Nectar of the gods," Stanley beamed, "for a pair of goddesses."

"Stanley," Mae said, turning away from Larry, "it's too early to start making an ass of yourself. Wait till you've had at least two beers."

Stanley had no talent for dissimulation. He flushed and bit his lower lip like a small boy fighting tears. Silenced, he started back to the grill. Unfortunately, he had to pass Lila. She reached out and took him by the arm.

"Stanley darling," she said, "you didn't even kiss me hello. Are you mad at me or something?"

Lila Connor lifted her inviting face, and Stanley Walters kissed it with the conditioned reflex of one of Pavlov's dogs. Immediately he realized what he had done and looked utterly terrified. There was a shattering silence. Everything was put back together by David.

"What I would like to know," David growled, "is how the hell Stanley rates special favors. I haven't kissed anyone hello yet myself."

David gave Lila a kiss that Nancy thought warmish, but then Larry Connor said clearly, "As the Bible says, a tooth for a tooth," and strode over to kiss Nancy with an ardor that struck her as not entirely pretended. Also, it seemed to reflect on Mae Walters, who had been closer at hand; but Jack Richmond corrected the oversight by promptly kissing Mae, and then everyone moved around kissing everyone and the party was reprieved, if not saved.

Soon after that the hamburgers began to come off the grill. Everyone began to stuff himself and make frequent visits to the keg; even Mae sufficiently unbent to enjoy the deliberate attentions of Dr. Jack, which had the intended effect of taking poor Stanley off the hook.

Shortly after eight, darkness set in, and a slivered moon appeared. The party began to swing.

It was some time after that—nine or ten or so—that Nancy found herself on a redwood bench with Larry Connor. Lila's husband had been drinking with both hands and getting more and more sober and sad and lost. Nancy had always thought of Larry as being lost. Lost in his love, which had turned sour; lost in his work, which had gone stale; lost in his hopes, which had evaporated. Larry should have been a poet, Nancy thought. At least he looked like one—hot-eyed and thin and dark, with black hair that was always a little shaggy. He made her think of François Villon. François Villon leaving the gates of his beloved Paris, never to be heard of again.

"How was Paris when you left it?" Nancy asked solemnly.

"What's that?" Larry Connor said.

"Nothing. Larry. I'm just a leetle drunk."

"Are you drunk enough to permit a neighborly kiss?"

He kissed her before she could think, and she was

astonished and touched at the quality of the kiss, which was brief and tender and did not threaten other intimacies which would have had to be rejected.

"You're a sweet girl, Nancy," Larry Connor said. "I wish I were David."

"Why should you wish you were David? David is probably off somewhere kissing Lila."

"In that case, God help David."

"Oh, come off it, Larry. Lila's a beautiful gal. She looks so much like Natalie Wood it's disgusting."

"Does she? I hadn't noticed. I've sort of lost the capacity to notice things. Or to feel things."

"Poor old Larry. Positively decrepit."

"All right, it sounds pretentious. But it's true. I've been thinking about F. Scott Fitzgerald lately," the accountant said suddenly.

"Maybe you should ask Jack to give you something for it." Nancy giggled.

"Maybe I should at that. Fitzgerald had a kind of theme, you know. That the saddest thing in life is the diminishment of the ability to feel intensely. Lesion, he called it. The lesion of vitality. Just listen for a minute, Nancy. What do you hear?"

Nancy listened. But her head was whirling a little, and all she could hear was a pleasant singing in her ears that was partly personal music and partly the hi-fi that Jack Richmond had channeled to the terrace from inside the house.

"Nothing much," she said.

"That's what I mean. There are a thousand sounds around us, if we could only hear them. You remember how it was on a night like this when you were growing up? I used to sit and isolate each sound and listen to it separately. It was an intensely sad, almost torturing experience—a kind of bitter, wonderful ecstasy. But it's all seeped away. I remember, but I don't hear or feel any more."

"Keep trying, Larry. It will come back."

"It won't. Not ever."

Larry sounded so peculiar that Nancy began to feel uneasy. At the same time, she became aware of a compulsion to pull his shaggy head to her breast. This compulsion she successfully quelled. It was chiefly an effect of the beer, she told herself, and it could lead to something dangerously more than motherly tenderness. So she merely waited for Larry to continue.

"Do you know how Lila and I met?" he asked. "Has Lila ever told you?"

"No."

"It's just as well. Anything she'd have told you would almost certainly be a lie."

"Larry, you mustn't say such things about Lila. You're drunk, or you wouldn't."

"*In vino veritas,* or whatever the hell the word is for beer," Larry said with a laugh. "Lila's the world's slickest liar. Didn't you know that, Nancy? It took me quite a while to get on to it. What's more, she's a psychopathic liar. She actually prefers lying to telling the truth. She has no conscience, no sense of the difference between right and wrong. She's sick in the head, Nancy, and there's no cure for it except to put her out of her misery, the way you'd shoot a rabid dog."

If Larry Connor had *sounded* drunk, Nancy would simply have jumped up from the bench and gone away. But he did not sound drunk. On the contrary, he sounded cold stone sober, even deliberate, as if he were thinking a serious problem out aloud.

"You mustn't say things you'll be sorry for later, Larry," Nancy said. "There's Lila and Jack. Let's join them."

She started to get up from the redwood bench, but Larry seized her hand and pulled her back. She was not aware until later that he held on to her all the while he was talking.

"Wait a minute, Nancy, I was going to tell you how Lila and I met. It was in Kansas City. I was in an office there with two older accountants, and everything was going fine. There was even a girl I was thinking about marrying. Then I went to this cocktail party one night and met Lila. She was sitting by herself in a corner with a Martini in her hand. I went over and began to talk to her. We left together and had dinner and went on to her apartment. She began to tell me about herself. She had just got a divorce, she told me, from a sadist who'd got his kicks out of making her suffer. I was furious and protective, and I built up quite a hate for the poor slob.

"None of it was true. I met him after Lila and I had been married about a year, and he turned out to be as nice a guy as you'd ever want to meet. Furthermore, he hadn't been her first husband, as she claimed. He'd been her third; I'm her fourth, and she's only twenty-six *now*. She started early, at sixteen. She'd been divorced by husbands one and three. Number two committed suicide."

"Larry, you simply must stop. I don't want to hear any of this."

"Don't you believe me?"

"I just don't want to *listen*."

"Please, Nancy. You're the only one here I give a damn about. I'd like you to know so you'll understand anything that may happen later."

"Don't *talk* like that, Larry. You're scaring me!"

"No, no, I don't mean to frighten you. It's a kind of therapy to be able to talk, Nancy. Please, let me. Have you ever wondered why Lila and I moved here a year or so ago?"

Nancy settled back. "You came to take over old Mr. Campbell's business, didn't you? I heard that you bought into it just before he died."

"The truth is that I thought Lila and I could start over in a small town. She'd run up about ten thousand dollars' worth of bills I couldn't pay, even though I had a good income. I thought maybe she'd be different here. She isn't. I still owe about half the Kansas City debt, and she's getting me over my head in debt all over again. I'm half out of my mind, Nancy. Maybe I'll just cut and run."

"Running wouldn't do any good, Larry." Nancy was terribly uncomfortable.

"I wonder. Sweet neighbors you've got, Nancy."

"We think so. David and I both," Nancy murmured fatuously.

"That's because you didn't know the truth, and probably don't believe it now that you've heard it. Thanks, anyhow."

"Yes, Nancy," Lila's voice said suddenly from behind the bench. "It's kind of you to say so. Larry darling, have you been entertaining Nancy with your drunken fantasies? Why is it you're always impelled to tell such monstrous lies when you're stoned?"

Nancy jumped up, startled and ashamed. Lila Connor was regarding her husband with the strangest smile. Jack Richmond, beside Lila, was wearing the professional expression of his consulting room. Larry merely shrugged, not bothering to turn his head.

"Must you sneak up behind me like that, Lila? I was just telling Nancy what a psychopath you are."

"I heard you. Nancy, you'll have to forgive him. He'll say or do anything to gain a little sympathy from a pretty woman."

"Forget it," Jack Richmond said. "Let's have another beer."

"I think we'd better not," Lila said. "I think we'd better go home. Don't you think we'd better go home, Larry?"

"Yes." Larry sighed and rose, a picture of defeat and weariness, as if he had lost and lost and lost again. "Good night, Nancy, Jack. Next time, Jack, be more discriminating in your guest list."

The accountant walked off into the darkness beyond the terrace toward his house. From Lila Connor came a brittle little laughing sound. She seemed about to say something. But then she raised her arms, and dropped them, and walked off after her husband.

"Well," Jack said, "they've done it again. What in the world was all that babbling about, Nancy? I only heard a bit at the last."

"I'd rather not discuss it, Jack."

"Right," the doctor said instantly. "Let's go see if we can stamp out more fires, Nancy. I think Mae's lighting into old Stanley again."

But Mae and Stanley Walters were in a truce for a welcome change, and soon, without further incident, the Walterses said good night and went home across the alley. Jack and David had a last beer while Nancy helped Vera clean up the terrace; then Nancy and David went home, too, across the Connors' backyard. Although it was still early, about eleven o'clock, they saw only one light in the Connor house, coming from a room upstairs.

3

"Darling," Nancy Howell said, "what do you think of Lila?"

"She's beautiful, sexy and delightfully promiscuous," David Howell said. "I discovered it tonight behind a spirea bush. The promiscuous part, I mean."

David was lying on his side with his back to Nancy, who was sitting on the opposite side of the bed in a pale yellow shortie nightgown. There was only a dim light burning, the lamp on the bedside table, because David wanted to go to sleep, which was why he had his back turned and why he said what he did in answer to Nancy's question. What he said was supposed to be a stopper; and what he meant, instead of what he said, was, in effect, to quit-talking-for-God's-sake-and-turn-out-the-light-and-get-to-sleep. Unfortunately, Nancy wasn't sleepy in the least.

"I guess that was when Larry and I were making love on the redwood bench," she said. "Really, though, David. What *do* you think of Lila? I mean *really*. What you think, I mean, when you don't intend to tell anyone, at all, ever."

"I just told you."

"Larry said she doesn't know the difference between right and wrong."

"Larry's right. She has absolutely no morals, I'm happy to say."

"Larry says she's a natural-born liar."

"I'm all for lying myself," said David, sleepily. "Like you, for instance, lying right now—lying down and turning out the light. Good night, lover."

"Lover! I can't even keep you awake."

"It's too soon after Lila, lover. Contact me first thing in the morning."

"Aren't you even interested in what Larry said?"

"Larry was drunk. What a man says when he's drunk is seldom interesting."

"I'm not so sure Larry was drunk. He didn't talk or act drunk."

David's response was a deliberate snore, which meant that he was damned if he was going to say another word. So Nancy sat quietly on the edge of the bed thinking over Larry's evaluation of his wife. Nancy didn't want it to be true, for she genuinely liked Lila. On the other hand, she didn't want it to be untrue, either, for she liked Larry just as genuinely.

Pretty soon David began to breathe as if he was actually asleep instead of pretending to be. Nancy went into the bathroom. She turned on the little nightlight in the outlet above the mirror where you plugged in your electric razor if you used one, which David didn't; then, leaving the bathroom door open, she came back, turned off the bedside lamp, and returned to the bathroom. She squeezed a ribbon of paste onto her toothbrush and brushed her teeth vigorously; then she sat down on the edge of the tub and wondered what a girl did when her husband wasn't interested in anything interesting—conversation or otherwise. She could, of course, go downstairs and make herself a sandwich which she didn't want, or a cup of coffee which would only push sleep farther off. So those were out. To be honest, her head was not quite stable from the beer, and what she really ought to do was to go outside and walk around in the fresh night air.

Having decided what she ought to do, Nancy proceeded to do it. She stole back into the bedroom, found the shirt, shorts and flats she had worn to the party, returned to the bathroom, removed her shortie, and redressed. Then she went downstairs and out the front door. The silver of moon was gone in a luminous sawdust of stars, and a soft breeze blew from the west. Altogether it was as pleasant a night as a wife with a sleeping husband could ask.

She sat on her front steps for a while, then strolled down the walk to the street. Turning left, she sauntered along looking up at the stars. She had just reached the Connors' driveway on the far side of their front yard when, suddenly, the door of their attached garage rolled up with a clatter, and there, in the light of his garage, stood Larry Connor. As Nancy watched he got into his car, a Buick Special, started the engine, and backed out. Nancy saw him stop in the drive, get out of the car and turn off the garage light, and pull the door down. In the Buick again, he backed slowly down the drive to the street. When he came even with Nancy on the sidewalk, she spoke to him, although, until that instant, she hadn't had the least intention of doing so.

"Hello, Larry," Nancy said. "Where are you going?"

Larry braked the Buick violently and leaned out his window, peering.

"Oh, it's you, Nancy," he said. "What are you doing out here at this time of night?"

"I couldn't sleep and came out for a walk."

"Well, it's a nice night for it." Larry sounded reserved, almost formal.

"Isn't it, though? There must be a million stars, and the breeze is wonderful."

"Did you ask me where I'm going?" he asked brusquely.

"I guess I did, Larry, come to think of it."

"Well, I'm going down to my office to sleep. I go there to sleep when I find it impossible to sleep at home."

This sounded ominously like a reference to the Connors' domestic difficulties. Nancy kept still in the hope that Larry would change the subject, or go away. He did neither.

In the silence Nancy became conscious of an odd rhythmic sound that she could not identify. It turned out to be Larry pounding on the steering wheel with a kind of cadenced desperation. This lasted for only a few seconds, then Larry spoke quietly.

"You remember what I said tonight, Nancy?"

"About what?"

"About wanting you to understand how things really are?"

"I guess so. Yes—"

"You remember that. Good night, Nancy."

"Good night, Larry. See you tomorrow?"

"I don't think so. Maybe."

He backed into the street and turned and drove off toward town. Now, damn it, Nancy thought, he had her so upset again that she couldn't possibly go to sleep, just when she had begun to think that she could. She wished to hell that Larry Connor would have the kindness not to say things that might mean something or nothing or *everything*.

Nancy walked back and sat down on her front steps again and tried to decide just what Larry had meant by what he had said. Whatever he had meant, it was evident that he and Lila had had more trouble after getting home from the party, or he wouldn't be bound for his office at this hour to spend the night. Was it because he had talked to her, kissed her? Nancy decided that her feeling of guilt was absurd, because she had not really wanted either to be kissed or to listen, and had only submitted in a neighborly spirit.

After ten minutes or so, Nancy got up and walked around the house into her backyard, wishing she had remembered to bring some cigarets with her. Then she realized that her sudden craving for a cigaret had come from seeing a tiny glow in the darkness across the alley; in the Walterses' backyard. Someone was out there smoking. Stanley, of course; Mae didn't smoke. Poor old Stanley probably couldn't sleep, either.

Nancy walked over to the picket fence at the alley, peering through the darkness at the little red dot in the other yard.

"Stanley," she called softly. "Is that you?"

The burning dot jerked around.

"Who's there?" Stanley's voice said. "Who is that?"

"Nancy Howell. I'm here, at the alley fence."

The red dot drew nearer, and Stanley Walters took shape behind it. He was wearing a pair of pajamas with broad stripes that only enhanced his bulk. He leaned across his fence for a moment, as if to identify Nancy definitely; then he opened his gate cautiously and came across the alley.

"What are you doing out here alone, Nancy?"

"I couldn't sleep. It's such a lovely night, isn't it? Ever so much cooler."

"The weather report is for not quite so hot tomorrow."

"I hope so. The last few days it's been too hot even for sun bathing. Do you happen to have an extra cigaret on you, Stanley? I'm dying for one."

"Heaven forbid! A gal as pretty as you, Nancy, ought to live forever."

This was another of Stanley's attempts at gallantry, like the nectar-of-the-gods-for-a-pair-of-goddesses bit, but it didn't sound quite so silly here in the dark, so late, in a *tête-à-tête*. Actually it was rather touching, Nancy thought, because it was plain that poor Stanley meant every word of it. She took the cigaret he offered her and lit it from his, drawing deeply on it. The smoke in the cool starlit night was rich and satisfying, and to hell with lung cancer.

"Thanks, Stanley, you've saved my life."

"I'll come around later to claim my reward."

"You do that," Nancy laughed. "Couldn't you sleep, either?"

"No. Mae went right off, though."

"So did David. He's sleeping like a pig."

"Have you been out long?"

"A little while."

"I thought I heard Larry's car drive off a while back. Did you see him?"

"It was Larry, all right. He and Lila must have had a quarrel. He told me he was going to spend the night in his office."

"Larry shouldn't do that. I mean, go off and leave Lila alone like that."

"Don't worry about Lila, Stanley. She's been alone at night before. So have I."

"Larry thinks too much, is his trouble. He gets to imagining things."

"About Lila?"

"It's none of my business, but Lila doesn't deserve to be treated the way Larry treats her."

"How does he treat her, Stanley? I don't believe I know."

"You've heard the things he says to her. He just doesn't appreciate Lila properly, is all."

It was obvious that Stanley appreciated Lila, properly or improperly. Nancy decided that too much had been said about what probably shouldn't have been mentioned at all. Besides, she was getting goose-pimples, strange as it seemed after such a hot day. Shivering, she took a last drag on the cigaret and dropped it over the fence. Stanley automatically crushed it under the heel of his leather slipper. Pavlov's dog, Nancy thought.

"Well, I'd better be getting inside, Stanley. Thanks for the coffin nail."

"Think nothing of it," Stanley said. "Nighty-night."

About halfway to the house Nancy looked over her shoulder to see if Stanley was going inside, too. But he was still standing where she had left him. At first she thought he was gallantly watching her to the house, but then she saw that his attention was elsewhere. His head was tilted toward something above the Connors' backyard. Stanley was watching the lighted window of the Connors' bedroom! The room in which Lila was alone tonight, and apparently still awake. The notion that flashed across Nancy's mind was so fantastic that she had to laugh at it in the same instant.

Oh, no! Nancy thought. Even poor Stanley must know better than *that*.

She went upstairs. David was still sleeping soundly, the swine. Nancy got back into her shortie and crawled into bed beside him and lay on her back for a long time, resisting every temptation to move, or sit up and read or light a cigaret; and in an unguarded moment after this long, admirable exercise in self-discipline, she fell asleep.

4

In spite of having gone to sleep so much later than David, Nancy awoke much earlier. She was wide awake in an instant, feeling remarkably good considering all the beer she had drunk from the keg. The room was dim, the curtains drawn. She stretched and lay for a few minutes quietly, wondering what could be done on a Sunday that would be both amusing and inexpensive; then she got up and padded over to a window and opened the curtains. The front lawn was beginning to show patches of brown here and there because of the dry spell, and in a patch of brown near the walk lay the Sunday paper, the Kansas City Star.

Slipping a robe over her shortie, Nancy went downstairs and outside and picked up the paper. Stanley had been right about the temperature; it was cooler than yesterday. Maybe with luck there would be a rain later; the grass needed a rain. It would also need cutting soon if it rained, and David would certainly grumble about *that*. David didn't really mind cutting the grass; it was just that he had no confidence whatever in anything mechanical. He was convinced that all mechanical devices took on a kind of malevolent life the instant he attempted to operate them. If one of them started for him, he was amazed and incredulous; if he managed to complete a task without a breakdown, he felt that he had scored a major victory over the forces of evil.

Carrying the Star, Nancy went back inside. In the

kitchen she measured water and coffee into the perco-
lator, which she set to heating. While she waited, she
sat at the kitchen table and read the paper. First, with a
sense of civic and national duty, she scanned the head-
lines to see what was happening in town and Washing-
ton and Moscow and so on; but then she turned to the
section covering amusements, shows, clubs, concerts and
such, to see what was going on that she and David
couldn't afford. The coffee began to perc. Nancy poured
a cup for herself and sipped it while she went on to the
TV section and the book reviews—these constituting, so
far as she was concerned, about all of the paper that
was worth going on to, if you excepted the funnies and
the weekly magazine, which sometimes she looked at and
sometimes didn't.

Half an hour passing thus, she refilled her cup,
poured one for David, and went upstairs to the bedroom with a cup and saucer in each hand and the
folded paper clamped under her right arm. David was
awake, but groggy. He accepted his coffee with a grunt.
Nancy could see that his eyes weren't quite in focus yet,
so she didn't say anything, not even good morning, until
she had opened the curtains to the encouraging light of
the new day.

"Darling," she said then, "I must say that you were
quite a disappointment to me last night, especially after
we got home. Since all you were capable of was sleeping
and snoring, I was forced to go out and look elsewhere."

"Good for you," David grunted. "If there's anything
I admire in a woman, it's initiative." And he took a
grateful slurp of coffee.

"Aren't you even interested enough to ask if I found
someone?" Nancy asked peevishly.

"All right," said David. "Did you find someone?"

"As a matter of fact, I spent some time with Larry
Connor in front of his house, then I had a tryst with
Stanley Walters in the alley."

"You're absolutely insatiable, my love. How nice to have cooperative neighbors."

"Cooperative! Larry and Stanley were hopelessly inadequate. Larry had just finished having a fight with Lila and was on his way to his office to spend the night. The minute I told Stanley this, later in the alley, he began to speculate about Lila and showed no interest at all in me. Darling, you can be frank. Do I need a change of deodorant?"

"The way Brigitte Bardot needs a new bra," said David absently. "Forget it, cuddles. The boys just had an off-night. There will be plenty of others when they'll make you feel like a woman again."

"Do you think so? You're so good for a girl's ego." Nancy said suddenly, "Tell me, darling, what do you think of Lila? I mean, *really*."

David, who was propped against the headboard in possession of the book section, gave Nancy a wary look from the corner of his eye. She was seated on the edge of the bed in all innocence, but he was now sufficiently alert to recognize a loaded question. His reply called for thought. It would not do, of course, to depreciate Lila's assets too thoroughly, for this would constitute a childish denial of the facts and would therefore be subject to suspicion. On the other hand, a factual evaluation could only lead to trouble, no matter how clinically expressed. The best resort, David decided, was to badinage.

"You asked me that last night, and I told you," he said. "She's beautiful and talented and sexy. I don't blame old Stanley for speculating."

"I don't deny that she's beautiful and sexy, which anyone can see. But how do you know she's talented?"

"You mustn't forget, dear heart, that I spent considerable time with her among the spirea bushes last night."

"The only time I saw her in the spirea bushes, she was with Jack."

"That was *after* she was with *me*. After all, she does have breeding. She had to be courteous to her host."·

"*Please* be serious, David. Just for a *moment?* Do you think there's anything seriously wrong with Lila?"

Oh, no, thought David. You don't trick me with *that* ploy. He said, "I can't think of a thing, and I made a careful investigation."

"I mean psychologically, or something."

"How should I know? My investigation was physiological."

Nancy regarded her husband for some time. Then she said, pleased, "Oh, well, I can see you're determined not to be serious. Perhaps it's just as well. Are you interested in breakfast?"

"I'm interested in the paper. I suggest we have a big breakfast later. Then we won't have to bother about lunch."

Big breakfast later. This meant scrambled eggs and bacon and hashed brown and toast and jelly and coffee. It also meant that David was not going to be home at lunch time and was too chicken to tell her so straight out.

"What do you have in mind to do today?" Nancy asked casually.

"Do? I have in mind to read this newspaper, if you'll only let me."

"I don't mean now. I mean later."

"Later? Oh! Well, Jack Richmond did ask me to play golf with him today. Of course, I didn't give him a definite yes. Would you mind, baby?"

"Not at all," said Nancy coolly. "There is nothing a wife likes better than being deserted by her husband on Sunday, especially after he's hardly been home all week."

David slammed down his paper, glaring. "Well, damn it, you're hardly being deserted if I take a couple of hours to play a few holes of golf!"

"I know what, dear. Why don't Vera and I go along with you and Jack and swim in the pool?"

"Because Vera doesn't want to go, that's why! And if you're going to make a federal case of it, I don't, either!"

"Oh, *no*, darling. I wouldn't *hear* of your staying home. I wouldn't *dream* of standing between you and your golf. I'll just take a nap or a nice walk or something else exciting."

David said a four-letter word.

She began her walk by going into the bathroom. She came out, bathed and dressed, about ten minutes later and made a point of ignoring David, who had his still quivering nose deep in the book section and made a point of ignoring being ignored. He was already acquiring his martyred look, and Nancy knew that he would soon come looking for her and say that he had decided he didn't want to play golf after all, whereupon she would be sweet and say that of course he *must* play, he had so few exclusively male pleasures. They would argue lovingly about this for a while, and eventually he would depart for the golf course happily, full of a big breakfast, and she wouldn't really mind, although of course women had to make an issue of this sort of thing as a matter of principle. The truth was, she was feeling mildly guilty. David didn't really get to play golf very often, not being able to afford the country club, which Jack Richmond could, and so when Jack invited David to play . . .

It was getting hot again, although not so hot as yesterday. Nancy went into the backyard and strolled about looking at this and that; then she went back inside and had another cup of coffee. Whereupon David came downstairs and kissed her and said he'd decided not to play golf after all, Nancy not failing to notice that he had dressed in clothes appropriate to golf just in case matters turned out as they were both quite sure matters would. And as, in fact, they did. She fixed the big breakfast, David eating heartily; and then off he went across the Connors' backyard with his silly toys, leaving her to clean up the kitchen and consider what to do with her afternoon.

It kept getting hotter, a perfectly still heat, with not a breath of breeze. Seated in her kitchen under the window fan, Nancy began to feel sorry for herself all over again, especially when she thought of David after his golf having several cold beers in the country club bar. Nancy hoped she was a reasonable wife, but there was absolutely no reason why she should have to suffer from the heat. David couldn't afford central air-conditioning, true; but surely he could manage another window unit or two, so that the downstairs could be cooled, at least part of it? She had even spoken to him about this. But David had said he didn't see any sense in investing in more window units when maybe they could have it done right later, through the furnace ducts. This was sensible, she supposed—particularly if you could go off to play golf and drink cold beer in a cool bar.

Looking out toward the little terrace behind the Connors house, she began to think about Lila again, and suddenly it struck her that she had not seen a sign of Lila all morning. Even if Lila had slept late in her nice cool house, surely she was awake by now. It was after one o'clock. Probably, also, Lila needed cheering up, what with Larry having slept at the office and all, and would welcome someone congenial and female to talk with. In spite of what Larry said, Lila *was* good company at the times when she wasn't giving people that sort of uneasy feeling, and anyway the chances were that Larry had exaggerated their fight last night, made far more of it than it really warranted. All in all, Nancy couldn't see why it wouldn't be all right to go over and visit, especially if she took something along. A pitcher of gin-and-tonic would be pleasant to share on an afternoon like this, and it would effectively mask Nancy's ulterior motive, which was simply to spend the rest of the steaming afternoon in Lila's lusciously air-conditioned house.

Carrying the pitcher, Nancy crossed her yard and stepped over the low hedge into the Connor yard.

She rang. She rang again. Again. No one answered.

Exercising the prerogative of a neighbor with a pitcher of gin-and-tonic to share, Nancy opened the front door and stepped inside.

"Lila?"

There was no reply.

Suddenly Nancy was aware of the oddest sort of feeling. Something was wrong. But what?

Of course! The house was hot—the air-conditioning was off. Lila must have gone out somewhere, and Larry hadn't come home.

Still with the odd feeling, Nancy stepped outside, shut the door and went home again with her pitcher. Back in her kitchen, under the hot breath of the fan, she poured herself a glass of gin-and-tonic and began to drink it. Where in the world could Lila have gone? She hadn't merely stepped out for a few minutes, or she wouldn't have turned off the air-conditioning. Besides, the house was so hot that the air-conditioning must have been off for several hours, at least. Could it be that Lila had left for *good?* Last night, after Larry left the house? Or early this morning? But in that case, wouldn't she have locked the door? Although it was true that if Lila were angry or very upset she might simply have walked out without thinking or caring about locking up.

Nancy suddenly recalled how Stanley Walters, last night in the alley, had stood looking up at Lila's lighted window. Could Stanley have seen something that might explain Lila's absence. It wasn't likely; but *if* he had, he would unquestionably have told Mae, and Mae, of course, would be only too glad to repeat it on a world-wide broadcast—especially if it was about Lila, and most especially if it was something juicy. Nancy considered running across the alley to find out if Mae Walters knew anything, but not very seriously. It was too hot and too much trouble, Mae having nothing to offer in the way of central air-conditioning. It would be easier to telephone, Nancy decided. So she refilled her glass and carried it into the little front hall to the telephone. There was a small floor fan in the hall, and as she dialed, Nancy let the air blow on her bare legs and sort of skitter up onto her neck and face.

Across the alley, the Walterses' phone rang once. It was promptly answered.

"Hell?" Mae said.

"Mae," Nancy said. "Are you keeping cool?"

"Who is it?"

"Nancy."

"I *thought* I recognized your voice. I'm hotter than hell, if you want the truth."

"So am I. Maybe it'll rain and cool off."

"Well, there are some clouds over in the west."

"There are? I hadn't noticed."

"I certainly hope it rains and cools off."

"So do I. Oh, what I really called about, Mae, was to ask if you know where Lila is."

"Lila? No, I don't know, Nancy, and what's more, I couldn't care less. Isn't she home?"

"No. I was just over there."

"Well, I haven't seen her since last night."

"Mae, their air-conditioner is off. The house is so hot it must have been off a long time."

"So what? Look, Nancy, I don't know anything about Lila Connor, and I have no *desire* to know. Is Larry gone, too?"

"Yes."

"I wouldn't blame him if he's walked out on her. Not that he would. He'll prob'ly come crawling back to her on his stomach. Why don't you ask *him* when he gets home?"

"Maybe I will. Well, I've got to hang up, Mae."

"Goodbye, dear. Don't worry about the likes of Lila Connor. That kind always know how to take *very* good care of themselves."

Cradling the telephone, Nancy raised her glass. It was now almost empty, for she had been taking generous swallows during the conversation. She wandered back to the kitchen and sat down at the table again under the hot breath of the window fan.

Now what? Damn it all, it was only two o'clock.

Having noticed the time on her oven clock, Nancy was reminded that she had better put the roast in for dinner. David would probably get home between four and five, howling for his food after all that exercise and cold beer. Well, why not? thought Nancy. An early dinner would leave the evening free . . . just in case something interesting turned up. Meanwhile, here was the pitcher of gin-and-tonic, and no one to drink it with. David didn't approve of her drinking alone; he said it was a bad habit that could easily lead to alcoholism. But would it hurt if she had, well, just one more before putting the pitcher into the fridge?

Nancy poured it and drank while preparing the roast for the oven. After she got the roast in the oven she poured herself just one little drinkie more.

But it was damn funny about Lila, she thought.

Where could Lila be?

5

With the roast in the oven, Nancy was at odds' ends. She wandered about the house, even going upstairs to make the bed; but all the while there was a little voice in her head that kept asking where Lila was.

"How the hell should I know?" Nancy said.

She was coming downstairs again from straightening the bedroom when the persistent little voice suddenly reminded her of what Mae Walters had said on the telephone. Mae had said something about asking Larry, hadn't she?

"That's right," the voice said. "She did."

"But he isn't home."

"Then show a little initiative. He told you last night he was going to his office. He's probably still there, sulking."

"I'm sure Larry wouldn't thank me for meddling in his marital problems."

"He might actually appreciate it. If Lila's left him and Larry doesn't know it, he'd be grateful to you for telling him."

Having been convinced by the little voice, Nancy determined to earn Larry Connor's gratitude. Conveniently, David having gone to the club in Jack Richmond's Corvette, the vintage Chevvie which was the Howell family's sole vehicle was available in the garage. To Nancy's gratification, it started immediately. She drove downtown, a mere few minutes' drive.

Larry Connor's office was on the ground floor of a small brick business building in mid-block on Main Street. The day being Sunday, she was able to park directly before Larry's office. His plate-glass window had his name on it in bold lettering. The monk's cloth window curtains were drawn.

Nancy knocked three times on the street door. The monk's cloth remained unruffled; the Venetian blind behind the street door remained closed. Well, what did I expect? Nancy thought; but on the chance that Larry might still be sleeping the sleep of the utterly miserable, she drove around the corner to the alley that ran behind the business block and up the alley to mid-block, where she turned off into the small private parking area. Startled in spite of herself, she saw Larry's Buick parked in his private space.

She got out of her Chevvie and walked across the alley and knocked on Larry's rear door. Still no answer; and when she tried the door, it was locked. He wasn't asleep after all. With his Buick in the lot, he was obviously hanging around the neighborhood somewhere, too heartsick or sullen to go home.

And what am *I* doing here? Nancy asked herself.

But in some inexplicable way she was committed.

Her first assumption was that Larry had gone over to the cocktail lounge of the hotel to take on a manly load; but then she remembered that on Sundays the lounge was closed. He might be killing time in the lobby, of course, reading the Sunday papers or watching television. She decided to look there after having a peep at Applebaum's Cigar Store, which was another favorite hangout for the temporarily homeless.

Larry was not in either place. Nancy even checked with the hotel clerk on the chance that Larry might have taken a room instead of sleeping in his office; he had not.

Well, I've done *my* duty, Nancy said to herself. He

was probably in one of the bars that violated the Sunday closing law; and if he was, he could jolly well make it home by himself, even if he had to do it on his hands and knees. She had gone to considerable trouble, Nancy thought, but there were limits to good neighborliness; knocking on the back doors of illegally operating booze parlors defined one of them.

So Nancy drove home and stowed the Chevvie in the garage and let herself in the front door. Checking the roast in the kitchen, she noticed a can puncher lying on the counter by the sink, from which she made the logical deduction that David was back home and drinking more cold beer, damn him; whereupon Nancy marched grimly out the kitchen door into the backyard and, sure enough, there was David. And not only David, but Jack Richmond, too—didn't he ever have a house call to make?—and they were *both* drinking cold beer, after having obviously consumed a large number of previous cold beers at the club. Nancy could always tell when David had been consuming a large number of beers because, at such times, he always had a cringing look when he saw her.

"Hello, men," Nancy said calmly.

Jack Richmond started to rise as a gentleman should, but the deck was apparently tilting. He sank back in the yard chair with a groan, and Nancy sat down in another after moving it pointedly to a place some distance from where her husband was seated.

"You want a beer, lovey?" David asked. He wore the cringing look, all right.

"No," Nancy smiled. "There's what's left of a pitcher of gin-and-tonic in the fridge. I'll have some of that, please."

"Permit me," Jack said gallantly.

This time he mastered the deck, though not without lurching. While he was gone the Howells sat in total silence. Finally the good Dr. Richmond came back with the pitcher in one fist and a glass in the other, walking on a tightrope. He carefully poured from the pitcher and carefully handed the glass to Nancy.

"Thank *you*, Jack," murmured Nancy.

"Think nothing of it, m'dear," said their guest with a leer.

"Why in the devil," growled David suddenly, "are you making whole pitchersful of gin-and-tonic in the middle of the day?"

"Because, darling," Nancy replied after a hefty slug, "I had nothing to do and no one to do it with. Except to drink, which is something you can do beautifully alone. I know, dearest, that's the way wives become alcoholics. Through boredom."

"Oh-oh," said Dr. Richmond.

"*Hell*," said David Howell.

"And did you have a nice golf game?" Nancy purred.

"Yes, we did!" her husband said. "We played eighteen holes, and I shot a ninety-two."

"Is that good, dear?"

"It's not bad for a now-and-thenner," he replied shortly.

"Oh, it's very *good*," said Jack Richmond.

"It must be exhausting to play eighteen holes of golf on a hot day," Nancy said. "I suppose it's practically essential afterward to have a large number of cold beers in the club bar?"

"It is far and away the most essential part of the whole business," Jack said enthusiastically. "Sometimes, in fact, the golf can be dispensed with entirely."

"What I would like to know," David demanded, "is why you had to make so *much*. Were you planning an orgy or something?"

"So much what, darling?" Nancy said.

"You know what! Gin-and-tonic, that's what!"

"Oh, it doesn't spoil, dear. It keeps perfectly in the refrigerator."

"It keeps better in the bottle!"

"But I was going to share it with Lila."

"A generous gesture," Jack Richmond said. "You couldn't have done anything to please Lila more. Lila is a great gin-and-tonic gal. In fact she's a gin gal, and to hell with the tonic."

"Like you and golf," Nancy said.

"Exactly," Jack said happily.

"Why didn't you?" David said.

"Why didn't I what?"

"Share it with Lila."

"She wasn't home, that's why, and to the best of my knowledge she still isn't. Have you two seen her?"

"No, thank God," Jack said.

"Which reminds me," David said, "that *you* weren't home, either, when we got here. Where have *you* been?"

"I went downtown to talk to Larry, but I couldn't find him."

"Is old Larry gone, too?" Jack asked.

"He flew the coop last night after the party."

"No!"

"Yes," Nancy said. "I saw him leaving."

"He'd had another fight with Lila," David said.

"Good for him," Jack said. "I don't blame him for cutting out. I only blame him for always coming back for more. If I were Larry I'd cut out for keeps."

"It's all very well to blame Lila," Nancy said primly, "but I'm not so sure it's all her fault. If you want *my* opinion, there's been far too much criticism of her lately."

Jack took a swig from his can, then shook it with an air of abstraction. He set the can precisely on the grass.

"Lila," he said, "is an avaricious, vindictive, cold-blooded *bitch*."

He said this in the kindliest professional tone of voice, a doctor making an unpleasant diagnosis. Still, it was a kind of shock. Of course, Jack had drunk quite a lot of beer.

"What *I'd* like to know," David said to Nancy, "is why you went downtown looking for Larry."

"Because I thought Larry ought to know Lila was gone."

"Damn it, what's so unusual about someone's being away from home? I simply can't understand why it concerned you. Are you sure that's the only pitcher of gin-and-tonic you've made?"

"I don't believe I would keep returning to that subject, David. I was concerned because their air-conditioner was off and the house was hot. It may seem reasonable to you for a person to turn the air-conditioner off when she's going out for a while, but it doesn't seem reasonable to me. I've got a feeling something is wrong."

"Turned off the air-conditioner, eh?" Jack said wisely.

"Oh, a fuse blew," David said.

"I don't think so."

"You say old Larry cut out last night?" Jack said. "I'll bet Lila cut out right afterward. The whole thing's blown to hell, if you ask me, and what we'd better do is let it strictly alone."

"That's right," David said. "Strictly."

"Do you think so?" Nancy said. "It may interest you boys to know that I disagree. I think we should go over and look through that house. As a matter of fact, that's just what I'm going to do, whether you two come with me or not."

"If you'll excuse my saying so," Jack said, "I think it would be a lot smarter if we mind our own business."

"Second the motion," David said. "How about another beer, Jack?"

"I—" began Jack.

Nancy said, "I'm going over right now. David, are you coming or not?" She rose grimly, waiting.

David sighed and rose, too. "Jack, help yourself to the beer. We'll be back in a few minutes."

"I may as well come along with you." Jack also rose, sighing. "As a good neighbor, I suppose I ought to get involved in any trouble you two get yourselves into."

They crossed the hedge, and Nancy went ahead of Jack and David through the back door of the Connor house onto a small landing from which three steps led up to the kitchen and six steps went down to the basement. Nancy suggested that the two men check the fuses in the basement, and waited for them on the landing. When they came back David said, "Nothing wrong with the fuses. The unit has simply been turned off. Lila's flown the nest, all right. Let's get the hell out of here."

Nancy said, "*I* am going upstairs and look in Lila's room, and that's all there is to it."

She did so, followed uneasily by David and Jack, but that was not all there was to it—not by far. They went through broiling rooms to the stairs and upstairs into a hall that was sizzling and down the hall to the door of Lila's bedroom. The door was shut, and Nancy pushed it open and immediately saw that her odd feeling of calamity had been right on the beam, as she had somehow known it would be.

Lila was in her room, dead. She was lying on the floor beside the bed, as if she had slipped off in dying, or had fallen against it. She was in a pale pink, translucent nightgown, and from its breast protruded the handle of what appeared to be a knife and which must, from its location, have pierced her heart. Around the handle, spread raggedly through the thin stuff of the nightgown, lay a dark seepage that looked stiff and dry.

Nancy felt as if someone had whopped her suddenly in the belly. She uttered a harsh wheezing cry that trailed off to a whimper and collapsed in her husband's arms.

"My God," said Dr. Jack Richmond huskily. "Old Larry's finally gone and done it. By God, Lila finally drove him to it."

6

When the doors to the offices adjoining the central room of the police station were open, as they currently were in the heat, any sound in the central room was shared by all, even by those who might have preferred to mind their own business.

When the telephone rang and the day desk man answered, Lieutenant Augustus Masters, hung up in his personal glorified sweat-bath, found himself automatically cocking an ear. Long experience in evaluating the nuances of the desk man's voice told the lieutenant that something of unusual gravity was being reported—a deduction immediately verified when the desk man buzzed the chief and asked him to take the call. Whereupon Masters also heard the chief's voice from the chief's office on the other side of the central room. At that distance eavesdropping called for concentration, and with a little extra effort Masters could have made sense of it; but he did not bother.

He did not bother because he knew that if the matter was of any importance at all he would hear about it from the chief practically at once. The chief of police, being full of years and approaching honorable senility, was a cripple in any police matter requiring mental competence, and Masters was his favorite crutch.

Now and then Lieutenant Masters thought with wistfulness of succeeding to the office of chief himself. But it looked as if the old man, unrestricted by a compulsory retirement law, would live forever. Anyhow, Masters admitted to himself, he couldn't possibly get the appointment. He had an unfortunate handicap—he looked like a clown. People always reacted to him as if he were about to take a pratfall or run face on into a custard pie.

Aware that the chief had stopped talking, Masters began to count to himself, spacing the numbers at one-second intervals. It used to take nine seconds, but the chief was slowing down with great rapidity; it took about fourteen these days. He had reached the count of twelve when the chief came in and sank into the other chair. Masters almost whistled. This *must* be a blockbuster.

One look at that seamed and lobster-colored face and Masters knew that the phone call had involved something not merely significant but catastrophic. The chief was plainly in a panic. It was a crying shame, Masters thought, that the local miscreants did not declare a moratorium on crime and leave the old man in peace until the morticians could decently get their hands on him.

"What is it," said Lieutenant Masters, "a murder?"

The old man's brow, which was as cracked as the sun-baked bed of a long-dry arroyo, suddenly became as blank as the top of his head.

"How did you know?" he exclaimed.

"I'm psychic," Masters sighed. "Who is it?"

The chief swabbed his face with an old-fashioned blue bandanna. "A woman named Connor, Mrs. Lila Connor. Lives out in Shady Acres. Her husband is Larry Connor, the accountant. He's missing and it looks like he killed her." For a moment the old man looked almost happy. "Seems pretty open and shut, Gus. Just a matter of getting a few details and making the arrest."

"After we find Connor, you mean."

"Naturally. They're pretty prominent among the

younger married set, Gus, so it'll probably be played for all it's worth in the newspaper."

"Well, this town doesn't often get a murder to play with. You want me to look into it?"

"It's the kind of thing you handle like a master, Gus. Anyway, it's open and shut."

"Thanks," Masters said dryly.

"You'll need to talk to the neighbors out there, but go easy on them. We don't want any complaints. The guy who called in was Dr. Jack Richmond—you know, John R. Richmond? Citizens like that can give us a hard time if we get them sore."

"I never get anyone sore, Chief, you know that. Lovable Gus, that's me."

"All right, all right, you better get on out there. I'll get hold of the coroner. Here's the address."

Masters took it and left. He was only slightly bitter; his laughter, churning his insides, was only moderately derisive. He drove over to Shady Acres in less than ten minutes, and in less than five thereafter he had found the house. Oddly, there was no sign of anyone.

He went around to the back, beginning to hear voices.

There were six people gathered on a flagstone terrace. They immediately stopped talking and studied the final steps of his approach with critical intentness. Masters was sure they were noting his resemblance to the late W. C. Fields and giving him demerits as a police officer accordingly. This did not disturb him. He had learned from experience that it gave him an advantage.

"I'm Masters," he said. "Lieutenant of police. Who's Dr. Richmond?"

"Here," Jack said.

"I understand you reported a murder."

"That's right. Mrs. Connor has been stabbed to death. She's upstairs in the bedroom. I mean her body is."

"Did you discover the body?"

"Yes."

"I was with him," Nancy said. "I'm Nancy Howell."

"So was I," David said. "I'm David Howell."

"Why?" Masters demanded.

"Because Jack didn't want to go," Nancy said. "As a matter of fact, neither did my husband. It was only when I threatened to go alone that they agreed to go with me."

"That's not what I mean, Mrs. Howell. Why did anybody go? Is it the usual thing around here to walk into other people's houses and look into their bedrooms?" The old technique, thought Masters; get 'em sore and they open up.

But beyond a few flushed faces, he evoked no reaction. They were apparently still too shocked by the murder. "Lila and Larry had a fight last night at the party," the pretty little thing named Nancy Howell said, "and then Larry left home afterward, and all morning and afternoon today Lila didn't show up, so naturally I was worried."

"So you came over here and barged into Mrs. Connor's bedroom."

"Not at all. It was nothing so simple. First I came over with a pitcher of gin-and-tonic, but I only stepped inside the back door, and the air-conditioner was off. I couldn't see any reason why it should be, and I began to wonder. That's when I decided to go down to Larry's office to see if he was there, but I couldn't get any answer."

"What made you think he might be at his office on a Sunday morning?"

"Because he'd said he was going there. Last night, I mean, when I saw him leaving in his car. He sometimes slept in his office when he and Lila had a quarrel."

"I see," Masters said.

He didn't, not clearly; but he had at least an unorganized impression of what had taken place, which he would try to organize after examining the body and the bedroom. In good time he would return to these neighbors gathered on the Connor terrace, the most promising of whom seemed to be the pretty scatter-brained young woman with the runaway tongue.

"Suppose you show me the body, Doctor," he said, turning to Jack Richmond.

"I'll go along if you want me to," Nancy said.

"I won't," David said, "unless you insist."

"One person is enough," Masters said. "Doctor?"

At the door to the murder room Jack Richmond stepped aside. Masters took three steps into the room and stopped. On the floor lay the woman, and sticking out of her left breast was the handle of the weapon that had killed her. She must have been a stunner, Masters thought.

"Has anything been touched in here, Doctor?"

"No. Nancy fainted when she saw the body, and David had to carry her back down to the terrace. I went immediately to the phone in the downstairs hall and called the police."

"You did just right."

Masters knelt beside the body and tested the flesh with his fingertips. The weapon, he noted, was not a knife but a metal letter-opener. The woman had obviously been dead for a long time. He almost asked the doctor for his opinion, but caution stopped him. Better to wait for the coroner's physician's report. Masters got to his feet and wiped his fingers on his handkerchief. He made a brief tour of the room.

"It's funny," he said.

"That depends on your sense of humor," Jack Richmond said from the doorway.

"Queer, I mean."

"What is?"

"This room. It's so neat. If she and her husband had a fight that ended in a killing, you'd think there'd be signs of a struggle."

"Not necessarily, Lieutenant. Larry was a strange sort in some respects. I rather imagine, when he was finally driven to it, that he went about it quietly. He probably just got the letter-opener and used it before Lila realized what he was up to."

"You seem awfully sure he's guilty, Doctor."

"It's certainly indicated, isn't it? He's run away, and who else could have done it?"

Masters grunted. "What makes you think the weapon is a letter-opener?"

"Because, from the looks of the handle, that's what it is."

"That's right, it is. You have good eyes, Doctor. I wonder why the air-conditioning was turned off. Any ideas about that?"

"Yes. By the time they got home last night the weather had turned much cooler. I imagine they meant to open some windows in their room here. Fresh air beats air-conditioning any time. My wife and I did the same thing."

"But no windows are open."

"They just didn't get around to opening them. Probably started to fight right off."

"That's good thinking, Doctor. Well, there's nothing more to be done here until the coroner and my fingerprint man get here. Let's get back to the people on the terrace."

Out in the hall Masters halted abruptly to stare at the wall beside the bedroom door, as if he had suddenly come upon a most astonishing thing.

"Is this the thermostat?"

"I think so. Yes, it is."

He reached up and with index finger slowly turned the dial which regulated the temperature. After a moment, through the air ducts, came a faint click of mechanism and whir of fan.

"It works," Masters said.

"Of course it works. What did you expect?"

"I thought something might have gone wrong with it. But it's working." He turned the dial back to where it had been, and the faint sounds stopped. "The thermostat must have been deliberately set so the air-conditioner wouldn't come on."

"Of course. Last night so was mine. They intended to open windows."

"Very logical explanation, too, Doctor. Well, we may as well go down."

On the Connor terrace Jack Richmond performed proper introductions, and Masters filed each away in his head with identifying tags. Stanley Walters was a jellyfish; he probably had a high susceptibility to pressure, malign or benign, and would cling and yield. His formidable wife, Mae Walters, had a low tolerance level; her influence on Stanley, with its system of restraints, gave their union little chance of permanence. David Howell was a likable guy with an open, scoured-looking face, but this was a good disguise for a man who might be quite otherwise. Nancy Howell, already tagged as a scatterbrain, nevertheless possessed an innocent sort of curiosity that, coupled with acumen, made her useful as well as a nuisance; a charmer, she was already a threat to Masters's objectivity. Vera Richmond, handsome and hefty in the hips, impressed him as a woman who accepted things as they were; she probably preferred being amused to being shaken up; her tolerance level must be as high as Mae Walters's was low. As for her husband, the doctor, he was simply too handsome to suit Masters, whose personal ugliness made him allergic to handsome men. In his experience such men were trouble-prone.

"I believe you said there was a party here last night," Masters said.

"Not here," Dr. Richmond said. "At my house, next

door. On our back terrace, to be exact. Just a few neighbors in for a barbecue."

"Which ones?"

"Those present here, plus Larry and Lila Connor."

"Did anything happen at the party that might explain what happened later?"

"Certainly nothing to make any of us think Larry would go home and do Lila in. No one would have been surprised to see them split up, but murder's another matter."

"So it is. You seem to have a reservation, though, Dr. Richmond. Please level with me—it may save us all a lot of time and trouble. Did the Connors have a fight at the party?"

"No. There was a delicate moment right at the beginning, but it didn't develop into anything."

"What was it, Doctor?"

Jack Richmond fumbled. Mae Walters promptly picked up the ball.

"What Jack means," Mae said, "is that Lila made a pass at my husband Stanley. She was perfectly shameless. She made a pass at Stanley every time he came close to her."

Conceding the maximum to Stanley Walters, and making allowance to women in general for their unpredictability in glandular affairs, Masters still found this charge incredible. He suspected that Stanley had merely been a jellyfish means of goading Mae Walters.

"Is that so?" Masters said mildly. "In front of seven other people, including her own husband, Mrs. Walters?"

"Lila was shameless, I tell you. She had the morals of an alley cat. I'm surprised Larry didn't kill her long ago."

"Please, Mae." Stanley spoke impulsively, certainly against his better judgment. "It's all right for you to make a fool of me, because I guess I am, but you needn't make Lila out to be worse than she was. It was just her way, that's all. It didn't mean a thing."

"Yes, darling," said Vera Richmond, "you mustn't exaggerate. You know perfectly well that all Lila did was to give Stanley a meaningless kiss. As a matter of fact, Lieutenant, it started us all off kissing one another immediately; and I must say, Mae, you seemed to enjoy it as much as the rest of us."

Mae Walters glared.

"Did anything else happen I ought to know about?" asked Masters.

"Nothing at all, Lieutenant," Vera said. "It was just a little backyard cookout. We didn't ask any gangsters."

"Apparently," Masters said, "you asked a murderer."

"Larry?" Vera frowned. "It may turn out that Larry killed Lila, but I for one refuse to think of him as a murderer."

This was such an arbitrary, if not downright preposterous, point of view that Masters was momentarily silenced. Nancy jumped into the breach with a certain air of reluctant necessity, as if she were doing an unpleasant duty.

"It isn't quite true that nothing else happened," Nancy said. "I mean, almost anything might turn out to be important in a situation like this, mightn't it?"

"It's a question, Nancy, of whether it's more important to talk about it or to keep quiet," Vera Richmond said.

"I'd prefer that Mrs. Howell talk about it," Masters said. "Yes? Go on."

"I was just thinking about what Larry told me on the bench," Nancy said. "Don't you remember, Jack?"

"I remember," said Jack. "I was hoping you didn't."

"Well, it was pretty grim when you and Lila came creeping up behind us and overheard part of what Larry said."

"We didn't creep. We walked."

"What I would like to know," Masters said, "is what was said."

"To tell the truth,'" Nancy said, "Larry was a little high on beer, and so was I. I didn't want to listen, but he insisted on talking, and there I was on the bench, trapped. What he said was that Lila was a psychopathic liar. He said she had lied when he married her—that he was actually her fourth husband instead of her second, which was what she had led him to believe. Her first and third husbands, he said, had divorced her. The second had committed suicide. She almost ruined him in Kansas City, where they lived before moving here, by her deliberate extravagance. That's why they moved here. Larry thought they could start over, but she was only doing here what she had done there."

"How much of this did Mrs. Connor hear?" Masters asked.

"I'm not sure."

"Most of it," Jack Richmond said.

"What was her reaction?"

"That's the odd part of it," Nancy said. "She didn't create a scene or even seem mad. Neither did Larry. They were both quiet and rather deadly, as if they'd finally come to the end of something."

"As," said Masters, "they had."

He turned away abruptly, tired of them all. But he turned back immediately, rubbing his hands on his thighs, and sat down on a redwood bench beside a table.

"I'll need to know, just for the record," he said, "what each of you did last night after leaving the party."

"As for me," said David Howell promptly, "that's no problem. I went directly to bed and to sleep."

"So did Stanley and I," Mae Walters said. "Isn't that right, Stanley?"

"Well, no," said Stanley. "Not exactly."

"What do you mean, not exactly?" Mae demanded.

"He means," Masters said, "that he didn't go to bed directly. Mr. Walters, what did you do?"

"As a matter of fact," Stanley said, "I did go to bed immediately, but I couldn't sleep. So I got up and went down to the backyard to smoke a cigaret. Nancy can verify this, because she saw me there."

"That's true," Nancy said. "I was dying for a cigaret, and I saw Stanley's glowing in the dark and thought he might have an extra one. I went over to the alley and called to him, and he gave me the cigaret, and we stood there talking and smoking for a few minutes. That was after I'd seen Larry leaving in his car."

"Are you brazenly confessing that you and Stanley were alone in the alley in the middle of the night?" Mae Walters cried.

"Yes, Mae," Nancy said. "I suppose I'd better confess everything. I said we only smoked and talked, but . . . wow-ee! It was love among the garbage cans, that's what it was. I'm sorry, David, but Stanley simply swept me off my feet."

"That's all right," David said. "Everyone is entitled to a little adultery now and then."

"Oh, now, that's too much!" Stanley protested. "You know perfectly well, David, that nothing like that happened at all. *Honestly*, Mae."

"Didn't it?" said Mae. "I'll have to think about it for a while."

"Please let's stop horsing around," Masters said. "Mrs. Howell, what time was it when you saw Larry Connor leaving his house?"

"I can't say exactly, but it must have been around midnight. We came home from the party about eleven, and David and I discussed a number of things, and then David went to sleep and I went outside. I sat on the front steps for a while, and after that walked down as far as the Connors' drive. It was then that the garage door opened suddenly and Larry backed out in his car."

"You spoke to him?"

"Yes."

"Did he sound upset?"

"He only sounded sad. He said what a nice night it was, with the stars and all, and that he was going downtown to sleep in his office. He said he hoped I'd remember what he'd told me at the party about him and Lila, because he wanted me to know the truth."

"That's all?"

"Yes."

"And I believe you said you drove down to his office this afternoon to try to find him?"

"That's right. David and Jack had gone off to play golf, and I had nothing to do. So I went to Larry's office. The front and back doors were both locked, and I got no answer to my knocks. As I told you, however, his car was parked in the little space off the alley. I assumed that he had walked off some place close. Now, I admit, Lieutenant, I doubt it."

"So do I. It's queer about the car, though. If he was running, why didn't he take it?"

"I'm sure I don't know. Perhaps you can find out."

Masters turned to Jack Richmond. "Now you, Doctor. Did you go to bed immediately?"

"No such luck," Jack said. "I was called out on a maternity case. A little past one A.M., it was. It turned out the patient's labor was prolonged, and I spent a couple of hours at the hospital waiting until I could deliver her. When I got home again I flopped into bed. I'm afraid I noticed nothing here to excite my curiosity, if that's what you're getting at."

"It is. Thanks."

The coroner came around the corner of the house, followed by two policemen, one in plainclothes, the other in uniform. Masters went to intercept them. Then he returned to the terrace. The officials went into the house.

"That's all for now," Masters said. "You folks have had a rough time. You'd better go on home."

He turned away at once and followed the coroner and the two police officers, presenting a rear view that would have instilled neither confidence in the innocent nor alarm in the guilty.

7

He left an hour later, with the coroner already gone and the pair of policemen winding up their work and securing the house. Evening of the long summer's day was drawing to a close, and Masters drove the short distance downtown with his headlights turned on. He made for the business block that housed Larry Connor's accounting office, turned into the alley behind it, and parked in the small area where Larry Connor's Buick still stood.

He got out of his car and went over to the Buick. The windows were rolled up and the four doors locked. He peered through the front window on the driver's side, but everything seemed normal. On the shelf formed by the top of the dash lay an open box of Kleenex, one of the tissues protruding from the slot. On the front seat beside the wheel was a crumpled cigaret pack. Nothing else.

Masters straightened, wincing at the stab of one of the minor back pains he had developed with the years, and walked over to the rear door of the building. It was locked, as reported. He trudged around, via the alley and the side streets, to the street door and tried it. Locked, all right. The lock looked capable. It would not open to any of the keys he carried, and breaking down the door seemed an arbitrary exercise of the police power. The landlord of the building would have a key, and Masters happened to know who he was. He went across the street to the hotel and used one of the public phones in the lobby.

The owner, whose name was Beyer, sounded unhappy on hearing Masters's request. But he agreed to come right over.

"Come to the alley door," Masters said.

He bought a ten-cent cigar before returning to his post. He did not light the cigar. He chewed it ruminatively, like a cow, as he leaned against a front fender of his car and waited. Beyer arrived with his keys in twenty minutes.

"Exactly what's the reason for this, Lieutenant?"

"Mr. Connor came here last night," Masters said. "His car is still parked here, as you can see. But he hasn't been seen since. We thought it might be a good idea to look into it."

"I don't like to trespass on the business premises of my tenants."

"I won't disturb anything without cause."

Beyer unlocked the door and stepped aside to let Masters go in first. Standing quietly in heat and stuffy darkness for a moment, Masters could hear nothing but Beyer's breathing, and see nothing but a vaguely bulky object ahead of him.

"There's a light switch on the wall beside the door," Beyer said. "To your left."

Masters groped for it. A pair of fluorescent tubes flickered and came alive near the ceiling. He was standing in a small cluttered room containing several large cartons and, lined against a wall, three metal filing cabinets. Obviously a storeroom for old records on their way to retirement. Ahead of him, in the wall he was facing, was a door with a pane of frosted glass.

"What's the layout here?" Masters said.

"Three rooms in a row, back to front," Beyer said. "The one past that glass door, the middle one, is Mr.

Connor's private office. Beyond that, just off the street, is a reception room where his secretary has her desk."

"I see."

Masters was now aware of a reluctance that savored almost of dread. He did not want to open the frosted glass door, which clearly he must. He found himself delaying the act, looking deliberately around the storeroom, into the cartons and filing cabinets. Finally he took himself in hand and opened the door. It swung inward, propelling a trail of light from the storeroom that picked out of the darkness the corner of a desk and the back of a chair beyond it. Masters reached in and found a switch, and a brilliant fluorescent ceiling fixture fluttered on, and in its light Masters saw what he had expected and dreaded.

"You don't have to stay any longer," he said to Beyer. "Just leave me your master key. We'll take over here."

"Why? What do you mean?" the man asked nervously.

Beyer peered over Masters's shoulder. He fell back with a gasp.

"Mr. Connor appears to be dead," Masters said. "That *is* Connor, isn't it?"

"My God, yes! But how did it happen, Lieutenant?"

"Looks like a suicide."

"This is terrible! Such a fine young fellow! Is there anything I can do to help?"

"Yes, Mr. Beyer. You can clear out and let me get to work."

He gently shut the communicating door to the storeroom in Beyer's face. After a moment he heard the man leave by the alley door.

Masters moved over to the desk and around it. At first glance, suicide was certainly indicated. Especially in view of last night's violence in the house in Shady Acres.

Against the wall he was facing stood a sofa upholstered in brown plastic. On the sofa, right arm trailing over the side, was the body of Larry Connor. He had

©Lorillard 1974

King Size or Deluxe 100's.

Micronite filter.
Mild, smooth taste.
America's quality cigarette.
Kent.

Kings: 16 mg. "tar," 1.0 mg. nicotine;
100's: 18 mg. "tar," 1.2 mg. nicotine;
Menthol: 18 mg. "tar," 1.2 mg. nicotine;
av. per cigarette, FTC Report Mar. '74.

Try the crisp, clean taste of Kent Menthol.

The only Menthol with the famous Micronite filter.

Kings: 16 mg. "tar," 1.0 mg. nicotine;
100's: 18 mg. "tar," 1.2 mg. nicotine;
Menthol: 18 mg. "tar," 1.2 mg. nicotine;
av. per cigarette, FTC Report Mar. '74.

Warning: The Surgeon General Has Determined That Cigarette Smoking Is Dangerous to Your Health.

made himself comfortable for death, Masters noted. His light cord jacket and tie were hung neatly over the back of a straight chair. His white shirt was open at the collar. He had not removed his shoes, which was the first thing Masters would have done in making himself comfortable, but his feet were resting side by side on the sofa in a position of repose. There was no weapon in evidence, no wound, no blood. Certain physiological signs suggested to Masters an overdose of some drug. Under the circumstances, suicide was strongly indicated.

He stood back and studied the office. It was almost square, about twenty feet in each direction. A frosted-glass door in line with the similar door to the storeroom obviously went to the reception room on the street side. Along the storeroom wall, near the foot of the sofa, stood a third door, half open, giving access to what was obviously a lavatory.

Masters went into the lavatory, fumbled around for a switch, found none, and finally located a chain hanging from the ceiling. He pulled this chain, and a single bulb flashed on. It shed rather weak light. There was a toilet and a washstand. Above the washstand hung a medicine cabinet with a smoky hinged mirror. On the washstand were the two halves of a small white drawer-type box, and a glass with a little water in it. On top of the water closet of the toilet stood a pint bottle of cheap brandy, capped, about three-quarters full. Masters picked up the drawer part of the little box and sniffed it. It gave off a familiar aromatic odor, now faint and almost gone. Masters had no difficulty in identifying it, for his knowledge of the shenanigans of the cheaper bars of the area was far wider than his experience with homicide. Chloral hydrate, the basic ingredient of Mickey Finns. In small doses it induced sleep. In large doses it brought collapse, coma, and coronary or respiratory failure.

Masters replaced the box and stood looking at the

brandy. He had not known Larry Connor, but he was nevertheless disappointed in him. Having executed his wife with violence, he had subsequently executed himself with a far tenderer concern for his own comfort. Taking the stuff in brandy!

Going back to the office, Masters helped himself to the use of the phone on the desk. He dialed the home number of the coroner, who had only just returned home in the hope of a late dinner. The coroner, an irascible man, did not respond kindly to this second summons within hours of the first, but he said he would come down at once. Masters hung up, then dialed police headquarters. He asked the man doing Sunday duty at the desk if the pair of officers he had left at the Connor residence had returned, and he was told that they had not. He asked if the chief was still there—highly unlikely; he was right, answer negative. He told the desk man where to send the two officers when they got back, and then hung up.

Masters sat down in Larry Connor's swivel chair, elevated his feet, closed his eyes, and chewed on his cigar.

Why, he wondered, had Larry Connor come down to his office to kill himself? After killing his wife, why hadn't he simply killed himself at home? Murderer-suicides usually acted against themselves in the same hot flush of rage and self-loathing that incited their murders. True, no pattern could be counted on. Suicides were always at least temporarily psychotic, each in his own way, and they often went off on unlikely tangents. Jumping out of windows and off ledges. Taking poison in public rest rooms. Slicing the wrists in hotels, where they had just registered for the express purpose. The variety of aberrant behavior could be as diversified as their particular lunacies. Larry Connor, fleeing his home without design, might well have not decided on suicide until after he had come to his office.

In that case, though, how had he come by the means?

Easily enough. Chloral hydrate was obtainable in any dive of sufficiently low character. Besides, wasn't the implication clear that Larry Connor had contemplated suicide before? Maybe he had already decided on chloral hydrate as a relatively pleasant means of dying and had laid in a stock, ready with a brandy mix. The questions were all academic now, anyhow. Larry was dead, for there he was. He had swallowed a massive dose of chloral hydrate, and that was that.

Masters heard the coroner at the alley door and went back through the storeroom to admit him. The coroner, small and sour and gray, hustled in and went sullenly to work; there was still a dot of gravy on his chin. Masters lingered in the vicinity of the alley door. There was a window, he noted, beside the door, separated from it by about eighteen inches of wall. Set in the bottom half of the window was an air-conditioner, a two-ton unit. The window was opposite the door to the office. The cooled air would be fanned directly through the office door if it was left open, thus cooling both rooms effectively. Masters was conscious again of the oppressive heat. He turned a couple of dials, the fan began to spin, and he felt the cooled air rushing in. He left the unit running and went into the office. The coroner was on his knees beside the sofa.

"What the devil have you stumbled onto," the coroner grumbled, "a vendetta?"

"Just a little family misunderstanding. You might have more trouble with this one. Anyone can diagnose a stabbing, even an undertaker, but this one is for the medics."

"It looks like a coronary, but under the circumstances I'd guess poison."

"My guess is that it was both. The former induced by the latter. The container is in the toilet there, along with the brandy he used as a mix. There's a faint odor in the box. You know what was in it?"

"What?"

"Chloral hydrate."

"An oversized Mickey Finn? Well, that would have done it." The coroner tore at his collar and tugged at his limp tie. "It's hot as hell in here. Can't we have some air?"

"There's an air-conditioner in the back. I just turned it on."

"I'm going to finish up here and get out, Lieutenant. Anyone else in this family?"

"No, just the husband and wife. Why?"

"I'd like to go home and finish my dinner!"

Masters went out into the reception room and located the light switch. The room was small, containing no more than the secretary's desk and a few chairs and a low table littered with magazines. In the transom space above the street door was another air-conditioning unit, smaller than the unit in the rear. One ton, Masters judged. How the devil did you get up there to turn it on? Then he realized that you didn't. The unit was left on all the time, being controlled by a switch lower down.

Turning off the light, Masters returned to the office to find the coroner telephoning. "Ordering ambulance," he said sourly, and nodded toward the collection of articles, from the dead man's person, on top of the desk.

Masters gave them his attention briefly. Coins, handkerchief, wallet, pocket comb, leather key-case, the watch from Connor's right wrist. In the wallet were twenty-two dollars, two tens and two ones, plus a driver's license, a few credit cards and some miscellaneous stuff, not significant. In the key-case were five keys. Masters frowned at them, then folded the case and dropped it into his pocket. The coroner, who had been barking into the phone, hung up.

"On their way," he said. "So am I. Here's the removal order. Let me alone for a while, will you?"

Masters said it would be a pleasure and listened for the sound of the night lock snapping into place as the coroner left by the back door. Alone, he sat down again in the swivel chair.

He had hardly settled his feet on the desk when he was startled by the kind of pounding that only a cop makes when he's outside wanting in. With a sigh, Masters got up and went to the alley door.

8

"You know," said Nancy, "he looks like one, and sometimes he acts like one, but I noticed that he doesn't talk like one. And in my opinion he isn't."

Lying beside David, she spoke in darkness. Her words gave the impression of round eyes. David had been breathing deeply, but he was not asleep. He remained quiet as he tried to follow Nancy's train of thought. It was, he decided, hopeless.

"Who?" he said.

"Lieutenant Masters. I've been thinking about him."

"Acts like what?"

"A kind of clown. A simpleton. I think it's his nose and the way his pants sag in the seat."

"Well, he's a lieutenant of detectives. That means he's supposed to be able to weigh evidence and make deductions and things like that. It would be fair to assume that he's not a complete fool."

"He's slimy, though. You'll have to admit that. Didn't you get the impression that he wasn't convinced that Larry killed Lila, in spite of everything?"

"No, I didn't. I got the impression that the conclusion was just waiting for evidence to support it. As soon as he finds Larry, he'll have it."

"You think so? I suppose you're right. It does seem pretty obvious. I guess I'm just hoping that Larry didn't."

"Sure. Poor Larry. He must have been driven hard to

make him go off the deep end that way. I wish I'd understood. I might have been able to help him."

"You think it's all true, then? What Larry told me
last night?"

"It must be. A guy like Larry doesn't go crazy over
nothing."

This remark seemed conclusive, and Nancy lay quietly
while David began to breathe deeply again. But she
was so unhappy about so much that she wondered if
she would ever feel like sleeping again.

"For all anyone knows," she said, "I might have killed
her myself."

There was sudden violent movement beside her.
David had shot up to a sitting position.

"What? What, for God's sake?"

"I said I might have killed her myself. For all anyone
knows."

"That's what I thought you said, and why the hell
did you?"

"It's possible."

"It's absolute *crud*."

"It's entirely possible. There I was, I mean outside
and all, while you were asleep, and I saw Larry leave.
I could have gone in right then and killed Lila, or I
could have come back and done it after talking with
Stanley in the alley."

"Oh, sure," sneered David. "You had a real motive,
didn't you? Lila cheating at bridge, I think?"

"I don't play bridge. You know *that*."

"Then stop fantasizing and get the hell to sleep."

"Maybe I had a real thing for Larry and hated Lila's
guts for what she was doing to him."

"Of course! And I never once suspected. Listen, Cleo-
patra, you couldn't *think* adultery without my knowing
it."

Oh, no? thought Nancy. "Well, anyway, I had the

opportunity, and I'll bet Lieutenant Masters latches on to it. *He* won't reject the idea, even if you do."

"I love you, damn it!" yelled David. "You're my wife!"

"Now, David, you know that has nothing to do with anything."

David was tensely silent, whereby Nancy knew he was counting to ten. "How long were you down in the alley with Stanley, did you say?"

"Oh, I don't know. Quite a while. We smoked and talked."

"You see what I'm getting at? I wasn't asleep at all. While you and Stanley were in the alley, I sneaked over and killed Lila myself. It only took a few minutes."

"You didn't even know Larry was gone."

"I saw him leave from the window."

"You did not, David Howell! You were snoring your silly head off. I wish you wouldn't make up such stories."

"It's no use," said David hollowly. "I'm making a full confession tomorrow."

Nancy lay down and rolled over on her side, and the feel of her rump made it clear that she wanted nothing more said about anything. David contentedly fell asleep.

"I think I'll go up to bed," Dr. Jack Richmond said.

"Let's have a nightcap first," his wife said. "I want to talk to you."

"Talk? Do you think that's wise, Vera?"

"It will probably be futile, but I'd like to try. It all depends on how honest you're prepared to be."

"All right. But I think you're making a mistake."

"I'll have a bourbon and water, please."

He left the living room and came back with two high-balls. He handed one to Vera and carried the other to the chair he had been occupying.

"Did Larry kill Lila?" Vera said.

"It looks like it."

"Where do you think Larry is?"

"I think he's exactly where you think he is. Or was. He's certainly been found, and probably removed, by this time."

"In his office?"

"Yes."

"Dead?"

"Of course. What other escape did he have?"

"You mean you think he commited suicide, Jack?"

"I'd bet on it."

"If you thought Larry was a suicide in his office, why didn't you say so to Lieutenant Masters?"

"Why should I? Let Masters find Larry himself."

"Do you think that policeman has enough intelligence to understand what happened?"

"Don't underestimate him. He's not the fool he looks like. As a matter of fact, I have the feeling he's a lot more capable than he *wants* people to believe. Don't worry about his seeing what's under his nose."

"You talk as if you *know* that Larry's killed himself."

"It's a logical assumption. The office was locked, his car was parked in back. Given Lila's murder, Larry's suicide fits."

"Well, that should pretty well close the affair, shouldn't it?"

"I hope so."

Vera sipped thoughtfully. "Still, you say Masters is bright. Suppose he's bright enough to keep on poking?"

"What about it?" asked Dr. Jack Richmond.

"I'm thinking about you."

"Me? I appreciate your concern, dear, but I can't see why that should bother me."

"Can't you? If that detective keeps on with his investigation, he may find out about your affair with Lila."

"We agreed not to discuss that again."

"I know, but all this rather changes matters, doesn't it?"

"It doesn't make me a murderer, Vera. The affair was over. I was completely candid with you about it, and you agreed to stay with me."

"Because you wanted me to."

"Yes, and I still want you to. I always will. Lila was a malicious bitch. She would have ruined me in time the way she was ruining Larry. Or rather, she would have made me ruin myself. But I put an end to it, and Larry never knew, and I'm glad for that."

"Are you sure it was over?" Vera asked, frowning.

"Are you starting to doubt me?"

"I don't mean you. Was it over for her?"

"She had no choice."

"Didn't she? Can a man scorn a woman like Lila and get away with it? She would have destroyed you if she could. As a doctor you're particularly vulnerable."

"Are you suggesting, Vera, that I might have killed Lila because she threatened my position in this town? I'm not such a fool or coward. There are all sorts of things I could do besides practice medicine. It would be tough, but it would be a lot tougher for me to commit murder."

"I wonder, darling," murmured his wife. "Anyway, I'm merely trying to read the evidence as a detective might."

"What evidence?"

"Stop and think. You were called to the hospital last night. You were gone over two hours. Where were you all that time?"

"I drove to the hospital, stayed there until I was finished, and came home."

"I know. You even called me and told me you'd be delayed. But can you prove that you were actually there all the time?"

"See here, Vera—" Jack began angrily.

"To make matters worse, you knew Larry had left home. Our windows were open and we heard him leave."

"What *is* this? Do you suspect me of having killed Larry, too?"

"There you go again, saying positively that Larry is dead."

"It's a logical assumption."

"Don't be angry with me, Jack," she said quietly. "I'm frightened. What would you do if you were accused? What would *I* do?"

Her distress dissipated his anger. He set his glass down and went to her and put his hand on her head as if she were a child. "You're a rare gal, darling. You're worth all the others put together."

"I love you, that's all. I shouldn't, but I do."

He grinned. "Thanks! Now, let's go up. I'll give you something to help you sleep."

"You go ahead, dear. I'd like another drink."

"I'll fix it for you."

"No, you need your rest. I'll do it myself."

He went upstairs, and Vera Richmond went into the kitchen and fixed the drink. She began to think after a while that she would like to move. She and Jack could well afford a better house in a more exclusive neighborhood. It had been difficult living here, with Lila just next door. Now that Lila was dead, it ought to be better, but somehow Vera doubted it.

Stanley Walters sat down on the edge of the bed and bent over his pot with a grunt to remove his socks.

"I don't see why we have to keep going over and over it," he said.

Mae's voice responded from the bathroom, its strained quality advising her husband that she was in the act of struggling out of her girdle.

"I'm sure you don't," she said. "I'm sure you think it

was perfectly proper for you to be down in the alley at midnight with Nancy Howell—in your pajamas. As for me, I have more decency than that, and David Howell would think so, too, if he had any sense."

"Well, you heard what David said. He didn't see anything wrong with it."

"I heard him, all right. I also heard what Nancy said."

"Oh, *nuts*. She was just breaking it off in you for making such a fool of yourself about it."

"Is that so? Maybe I'm not such a fool as she thinks. Nancy Howell is *tricky*, and *I'm* on to her if no one else around here is. She's just the kind who'd deliberately tell the truth in a way to make everyone think it was a lie."

"Mae. All Nancy did was call me over to the alley to borrow a cigaret, that's absolutely *all*."

"Was it?"

"I've said so until I'm sick of saying it!"

"I'm not thinking of what you may have done with Nancy. I'm thinking of what you may have done *after* Nancy left."

"I didn't do *anything*. Damn it, I came back to the house and went to bed!"

"That's what *you* say. I'm not so sure. I'll bet Lieutenant Masters won't be, either, when he gets around to thinking about it."

Mae emerged from the bathroom in her nightgown, and Stanley looked at her impressive approach with alarm.

"What's that? What's that supposed to mean?"

"Just what I said."

"Why should Masters doubt it?"

"If you can't convince your wife, Stanley Walters, how can you expect to convince a detective? Everyone around here knows that Lila Connor made advances to you every chance she got, and that you lapped it up like a—like a fish out of water. Nancy told you Larry had left home for the night. You've *admitted* that. I had taken a sleeping pill, which you also knew. So what was to prevent your paying a little social call on Lila while you had the chance?"

"Lila was dead. Larry killed her before he left. We know that now."

"Do we? It seems to me it remains to be proved. You haven't heard about Larry confessing or anything yet, have you?"

"Are you for God's sake suggesting that I may have killed Lila because she repulsed my advances or something?" asked Stanley excitedly.

"*I* didn't say that. *You* said that. *I* only say that your Don Juan tendencies have made you a suspect in a nasty murder case."

"By God, I like that! First I'm accused of making love to Nancy in the alley, then of sneaking over for a fling with Lila! You make me feel like a darned tomcat!"

"If I were you, Stanley, I'd just feel *frightened*."

Which, as a matter of fact, was exactly what Stanley was feeling.

9

Masters was at Larry Connor's office before eight o'clock on Monday morning. He didn't know what time the dead man's secretary reported for work, but he banked on the prevailing eight-to-five routine in town. He was right; it was one minute before the hour when he heard a key in the front door. Masters was waiting for her on the corner of her desk, hand shoved into a side pocket of his baggy pants fingering a lone quarter. The secretary was a pretty, well-set-up redhead in, he judged, her late twenties. She looked more surprised than alarmed when she saw Masters where he clearly had no right to be. Masters didn't much like her hair. The color was a good natural red, but the hair had been ratted before combing to give it an illusion of excessive body.

"Who are you?" she demanded.

"Lieutenant Masters. Police." He showed her his credentials.

"But, Lieutenant, why are you here? Is Mr. Connor in already?"

"No. He won't be in at all. That's what I want to talk to you about. You'd better sit down."

He drew his hand from his pocket as she moved past him to reach the chair side of the desk. She moved carefully, and he got the impression that she was anticipating very bad news. She deposited her purse in a drawer and sat down, folding her hands on the desk like a schoolteacher about to call a child to the blackboard.

"What's the matter?" she said. "Has something happened to Mr. Connor?"

"I don't believe I know your name."

"It's Ruth Benton."

"Tell me, Miss Benton, have you been secretary to Mr. Connor long?"

"Over a year. About fifteen months. Why?"

"That would give you time to have become pretty well acquainted with him. What kind of man was he?"

The true answer was visible in her eyes, and he understood that Larry Connor, whatever he had been to others, had been very special to her. Had she been to him? Quite possibly. Ruth Benton would look very good to a man who had a wife like Lila Connor.

"He was kind, and thoughtful, and honest. He wouldn't do anything dishonest, if that's what you mean."

"I don't. Did he show signs of emotional disturbance?"

"He had his troubles." She stopped, aware all at once of the tense Masters was using which, following his cue, she had used in turn without realizing it. "What has happened to Mr. Connor? *Is he dead?*"

"What makes you ask that?"

"Is he?"

"He is. He apparently committed suicide last night, here in the office."

She took it well; and Masters, who had been dreading her reaction, was grateful. He waited patiently, and soon she looked up and spoke quietly. The quaver in her voice seemed as much the result of anger as of shock and grief.

"So she finally drove him to it," she said.

"Who did?"

"His wife."

"Yes, I understand that he wasn't happy with Mrs. Connor. Was it that bad?"

"He's dead, isn't he? Isn't something bad when you'd rather die than live with it?"

"Do you mind telling me how you became familiar with his private life?"

"Larry told me. He had to talk to somebody."

So now it was "Larry," with no pretense. Masters rather liked her for it.

"You were friends?"

"Yes."

"That's all?"

"No." She stated it with neither defiance nor bravado, but as a fact. "We had a sort of special relationship. I'd rather not talk about it."

"I see. You met outside the office?"

"Sometimes."

"Where?"

"Various places. For drinks at the hotel. Now and then for dinner. A few times he came to my apartment."

"Thanks for being honest."

"Why shouldn't I be? We didn't try to sneak anything. We weren't sleeping together—it was all very innocent, Lieutenant. I wish now it hadn't been."

"Did he hate his wife?"

"I wouldn't say he hated her. She kept him in despair. He wanted to leave her."

"He took her with him, Miss Benton."

"What?" She gripped the desk.

"He killed her."

"I don't believe it!"

"Well, her body was found stabbed to death in her bedroom some time before his was found here."

Ruth Benton stared down at her clenched hands, and then she slowly lowered her head until her forehead was resting upon them. He waited for her to break, expecting a storm of tears; but again he was relieved. She rose after a few moments and retrieved her purse from the desk drawer.

"I'd like to go home," she said.

"Can I find you there if I need you?"

"I'm in the directory."

"All right, Miss Benton."

Clutching the purse she walked out, still giving the impression of rigid controls rigidly imposed. She was, he thought, a remarkably tough and durable young woman. Masters locked up and left.

At headquarters he reported to the chief, bringing the old man up to date on the two deaths and their apparent connection.

"It's a mess," the chief said, "but at least it's a *neat* mess. Murder and suicide. All in the family. Wrap it up."

"Before I wrap it up, Chief, there are a couple of things I'd like to look into."

"Why? What things?"

Masters dug into his pocket and produced the leather key-case that he had borrowed from Larry Connor's office. He opened it and laid it on the chief's desk.

"This key-case, for one. These two keys are to his car—one to the doors and the ignition, the other to the trunk. These two are to the front and back doors of his office. I've checked all four. This fifth one, I'm guessing, is to either the front or back door of his house. The point is, why didn't he have two house keys—to *both* doors?"

"That seems damn unimportant to me, Gus. Maybe the fellow just carried one key."

"True. Still, I want to run out to the house again. If you don't mind."

"You be careful, Gus. We can't afford any repercussions from this thing."

"The soul of discretion, that's me."

"You said a couple of things. What's the other one?"

"The air-conditioners. They were off at the house and office both. I wonder why."

"Damn it, a man planning to commit suicide would hardly bother to turn on an air-conditioner!"

"But what about the house? It was a scorching day. The air-conditioner should have been running. There should have been no question of turning it on or off."

"Maybe a fuse blew."

"It didn't. I checked. Dr. Richmond believes they may have intended to open their windows. The night had cooled off, and it's possible."

"That's it, then."

"Only they didn't get it done. All windows were closed."

"All *right*, Gus. Worry about keys and air-conditioners if you have to, but remember what I said. *You be careful.*"

Masters repeated that he would, and went across to his own office, where he found a memo from the man who had dusted for fingerprints. The report contained no surprises. Prints of both Connors had been found on various surfaces in the murder room. The husband's prints had been all over his office, including the box and bottle Masters had found in the lavatory. On the handle of the murder weapon, the prints of Connor's right hand had been found, no others. This in itself was not odd, but apparently there was only one set of them. Surely, even if Connor had been the only one to handle the letter-opener, he must have handled it many times. Why, then, a single set of prints?

Filing this slight puzzle away in his cluttered mind, Masters drove out to Shady Acres Addition. The Connor house on this quiet Monday morning looked normal and secure. He parked in the drive and cut across a corner of bluegrass to the front door. The key in the leather case fitted and worked smoothly.

He shut the door behind him and went upstairs. The

bedroom had been relieved of its only disorderly item, the corpse, and the officers had left the room as neat as they had found it. It was, Masters thought, an inviting nest for the exercise of conjugal love, and it seemed to be waiting patiently for love's resumption. Later, maybe, by others. Mr. and Mrs. Larry Connor were not in love, not at home, and not coming back. Masters sighed, reflecting on the waste, and went downstairs and let himself out, this time by the back door. He tried the front-door key on the back door from outside. It did not fit; it would not even enter the lock. Had there been another key in the case? If so, where was it?

Masters had the sudden feeling that he was being watched. He squinted sidewise and spotted a lusciously constructed young woman in white shorts regarding him intently from the terrace next door. Nancy Howell, that schoolteacher's wife. There was something engaging in her curiosity, which she made no attempt to conceal. In fact, there was something engaging in her every line and curve, Masters thought. An appetizing dish for a pedagogue to come home to.

He returned the key-case to his pocket and made for the dish.

"Good morning, Mrs. Howell," he said.

"*Good* morning," Nancy said. "I was just wondering what you were up to."

"Having another look. Sometimes you see something new when you come back."

"Did you?"

"I can't say I did."

"Have you found Larry yet?"

"Yes."

"I knew you would." She gave her shorts a needless tug, which had the effect of directing attention to her legs. But this time Masters was watching her eyes, which were equally lovely, and deeply disturbed besides. "He was right there in his office, wasn't he?"

"That's right. All the time."

"Dead?"

"Yes."

"Poor Larry. Poor Lila. I feel sorry for them both. I don't suppose you can understand that."

"My sympathy is usually for the victim, Mrs. Howell. But I've always got some left over for the offender."

"Isn't that an unusual attitude for a policeman?"

"Is it? To me, a person in trouble is a troubled person."

"What a lovely way to put it! It sounds like an epigram. Did you just think it up?"

"Probably not. I don't usually think in epigrams."

"Would you mind telling me how Larry died?"

"Not at all. It will be public knowledge soon. In all likelihood he died from a fatal dose of chloral hydrate taken in brandy."

"Chloral hydrate? What's that?"

"Knockout drops. Basic ingredients of a Mickey Finn. Harmless enough in small doses, fatal in large ones."

"What a strange thing to use!"

"Not really. It has advantages. It's easily acquired and easily taken. No pain, no sickness, no mess. You go into a coma, and that's it. Cardiac or respiratory failure. There are lots worse ways to die."

Nancy shuddered nevertheless. "Anyhow, this settles everything, doesn't it?"

"It would seem so. Murder and suicide."

"Then why have you come back?" She looked at him shrewdly, head cocked. "If everything's settled, I mean."

"There are odds and ends to gather up. Probably unimportant, but you never know. Besides, I want to ask you to do something for me."

"Oh?"

"Mr. Connor's body is at the mortician's. The law requires an official identification. Will you identify him?"

"Oh, dear."

"I shouldn't have asked. One of the men in the neighborhood will do. Is your husband home?"

"No, David left for the school long ago. And Jack's at his office, I should think, and Stanley's at his store. I'll go with you, Lieutenant. I . . . I don't mind."

"Thanks. I'll drive you there and bring you back."

"I'll get into a dress if you'll wait. Will you come in?"

"I'll wait here, thank you. No hurry."

Nancy returned in a simple blue dress that won Masters's admiration. He wondered how she had achieved such casual smartness in so little time with so few props. It was largely, he supposed, the result of basic assets, which were sound, very sound. All the way downtown he was keenly conscious of the little woman beside him in the police car, and he kept his eyes strictly on the road as a matter of discipline. What scent was she wearing? It was faint and elusive; and when he parked behind the mortician's, having approached through the alley, he still had not identified it.

Not so with the scent inside the building. It was the odor of death embalmed, and it seemed to seep from the very plaster and wood and old brick. Or perhaps it was only the amalgam of all the odors that accumulate where the dead are prepared for eternity. They were admitted by a man wearing a kind of apron; and he directed them to a small room where Larry Connor lay waiting patiently to be embalmed after his autopsy. Not, Masters reflected, that an autopsy in this case could reveal much of anything. Evidence of chloral hydrate, always difficult to detect, had surely dissipated . . .

He was aware all at once that Nancy had stopped walking, and he turned back to her. She was standing quite still, eyes closed and saucy face drained of color. He had an exorbitant feeling of alarm, certain that she was going to faint. But before he could reach her, she opened her eyes and took a deep breath.

"Are you all right, Mrs. Howell?" he asked.

"Yes. I got a little dizzy for a moment, that's all."

"Are you sure you want to do this?"

"I don't want to, but I will."

And it was, after all, not so bad. Larry was so still and remote, so withdrawn from all trouble whatsoever —and so essentially un-Larry-like, when it came to that —that it was impossible to feel more than wonder that he had come by his own wish to where he was. His sad thin face had fallen into lines of disdain that expressed his utter indifference to all that had happened to him or might happen hereafter. Was it only the night before last, Nancy thought, that she had sat with him on a bench and listened to him talking out of a keg? His voice returned to her in a whisper, come from an incredible distance and a long time past. And where was Lila? Was Lila also in this place of deathly sweetness? Nancy turned and walked away, Masters following. In the alley she stopped by the car, leaning against it for a moment; and he was aware of a desire to stroke her head, to hold her hand—to give her, by some human gesture, what comfort he could.

Masters was, in fact, feeling guilty for having subjected her to the ordeal. The truth was that he had been inexplicably reluctant to leave her, after their conversation on her terrace, and he had hit on this grim chore as a way of retaining her company. From the beginning of this affair, he had sensed that her lively and innocent curiosity was the product of a good brain, however scattered; and what he wanted to do, he now saw with considerable surprise, was to test on her the meager substance on which his uncertainty was founded.

"I wonder," he said, "if you would have a cup of coffee with me."

"I'd rather go home, I think."

"I'd appreciate it, Mrs. Howell. I'd like to talk to you."

"About what?"

"A couple of things that bother me. What do you say?"

"I'll give you a cup of coffee at my house, Lieutenant. Will that do?"

"If it wouldn't be too much trouble . . ."

So they went back and sat at the table in Nancy's kitchen and had the coffee that was left from breakfast. She watched him from across the table, her curiosity on leash.

"You may think I'm crazy," Masters began.

"Why?"

"Because, Mrs. Howell, this thing keeps looking one way, and I keep thinking it might have been another way entirely."

"What other way?"

"It looks like murder and suicide. I keep thinking it might have been murder and murder-made-to-look-like-suicide. By a third party."

Nancy was startled. "Whatever gave you such an idea?"

"As I said, a couple of things. A key that may or may not be missing . . . You finding the air-conditioner in the Connor house turned off. Why? Dr. Richmond thinks someone meant to open the windows. I'm not satisfied with that."

"But why else would it have been turned off?"

"What if someone had wanted to confuse the times of death?"

"I don't think I understand, Lieutenant," said Nancy, fascinated.

"In fixing the time of death with a reasonable degree of accuracy," explained Masters, "a number of factors have to be taken into account—the climate, the weather, the temperature, the barometric pressure, peculiar local conditions and so on. Bodies deteriorate much faster in high temperatures than in low, for example. Of course, where air-conditioners are involved the medical examiner takes them into account also in his figuring."

"You mean," breathed Nancy, "suppose somebody *manipulated* the air-conditioning factor in this case?"

Masters could only admire her quickness of mind. "Exactly. Let's assume a third principal in this affair, Mrs. Howell—and let's call him Murderer. Murderer wants to kill Lila Connor—let's not bother just now with why. He knows the Connors' domestic history; he knows they had a bitter quarrel Saturday night. He sees that Larry Connor is a natural set-up to be tagged for the killing if Lila Connor is murdered. Obviously, if he can frame Larry for Lila's murder, it's safer if Connor also dies and therefore can't defend himself. So Murderer says to himself: This has to look like a murder and suicide—the husband killing the wife and then taking his own life . . ."

"Are you seriously suggesting that Larry was killed simply to cover up Lila's murder?"

"I'm just thinking out loud," said Masters with a smile. "Now. Circumstances—maybe the pressure of time, or events that can't be avoided—make it necessary for Murderer to kill Lila and Larry Connor close enough together so that it would be hard, if not impossible, to establish with any accuracy *in which order the murders took place*. But the essence of Murderer's plot is that Lila's death be *medically recognized and accepted* as having occurred prior to her husband's. That's where the air-conditioning manipulation comes in."

"I see," said Nancy, frowning in concentration. "Or do I? Was the air-conditioner running in Larry's office when you found him?"

"No, it was off. The place was stuffy and hot."

"But if your theory is correct, wouldn't you have had to find Larry's air-conditioning *on?*"

"No. But let's not worry about the mechanics of it

now. The point is, Mrs. Howell, I'm not ready to accept the murder-and-suicide."

But Nancy shook her head. "It's too fantastic, Lieutenant. You have absolutely no reason for thinking all this. You've simply made it up."

"At least it would explain the hot house, and the missing key to the Connors' back door. If, that is, the key is actually missing. Do you happen to know if Larry Connor carried a back-door key?"

"He must have. I've seen him let himself in that way when Lila wasn't home."

"There you are. You're an observant young woman, Mrs. Howell. That's why I wanted to talk with you."

"I only hope that my observations don't make a lot of trouble for some innocent person."

"They won't."

"I'm not so sure. I'm beginning to think you may be just clever enough to think up something against someone who had nothing to do with anything."

"I hope not. Shall I go on with my fantastic ideas?"

"I admit they're interesting. As well as frightening. What's next?"

"Well, another thing that puzzles me is why Larry Connor would kill his wife and then deliberately go to his office to kill himself. Why not do it at home?"

"He couldn't have been very rational. Maybe he had some idea of running away, and later realized it was hopeless."

"I know, suicides often do crazy things. Still, it's something to be considered. You saw Connor leave. Did he act irrational? Did he act like a man running away from a murder?"

"No." Nancy stared into her cup, where the coffee was getting cold. "He didn't, as a matter of fact."

"There you are again, another little incongruity. All right, let's suppose that he left Lila alive. Suppose he was going, exactly as he told you, down to his office to spend the night. He could have been followed and killed, and the murderer could then have returned, bringing with him Connor's key to the back door, from Connor's key-case, and killed Lila."

"Wait a minute. This is getting more and more absurd. You are implying that the murderer, if there is one, is someone from right in this neighborhood."

"Oh, yes. If there is a murderer, as you say, he is surely right here in the neighborhood. Probably attended the party Saturday night."

"Which one of us, may I ask, do you suspect?"

"It could have been any of you. It depends on how much of the truth has been told. It may depend, too, on who is protecting whom. Think a minute. You say you left Stanley Walters at the fence in the alley after telling him Connor had gone to his office. So Walters is eligible. Dr. Richmond lives just on the other side of the Connors. He could easily have seen Connor leave, overheard the two of you talking in the driveway. Furthermore, the doctor admitted that he went out later on a prolonged call to the hospital. Did he go there directly? Did he stay there all the time? In any event, Dr. Richmond is also eligible. Shall I go on?"

"I'd rather you didn't," said Nancy faintly. "It's too utterly nauseating. The next thing I know, you'll be saying that I could have committed murder myself."

"Certainly. You're eligible, too." Nancy was stricken dumb, and Masters said hastily, "If I thought for a minute you were guilty, I wouldn't be talking to you this way."

"Well, I have talked with you far too long and said far too much, Lieutenant, and I don't believe I want to talk with you any more."

"I'm sorry."

Masters rose and looked wistfully into his empty cup, which he had hoped Nancy would refill. But she had risen, too, and was standing there, the very picture of womanhood offended. He said, to mollify her, "It's only speculation, Mrs. Howell." But when she continued to play Living Statues, Masters reverted to type and added, "*So far*, that is," and left with a bitter taste of triumph in his mouth.

10

As a suspect, Lieutenant Masters liked Dr. Jack Richmond best. In the first place, the handsome doctor's opportunity seemed—well, most opportune. In the second place, he was exactly the matinee-idol type that, psychically speaking, gave off the aroma of motive. In the third place, as a physician, he was in an ideal position to administer a fatal drug. Under the pretext of being concerned about his neighbor's welfare, he could have gone to Larry Connor's office, perhaps on his way to the hospital, and administered a "sedative" that Larry, upset by his conflict with Lila, would have taken without hesitation. Of course, a doctor would hardly prescribe chloral hydrate; on the other hand, a doctor bent on murder would use exactly the sort of drug that *wouldn't* be expected of a doctor. At any rate, it would be interesting and possibly informative to check into Dr. Richmond's purported hospital call; and Masters set out to do just that.

It was, of course, the wrong time. No one on duty in the hospital had been there in the early hours of the morning. All Masters could do was to check at the desk in Maternity to see if Dr. Richmond had reported in and out, which he had: in at 1:20 A.M., out at 3:30 A.M. A perfect alibi if it held up. Plenty of free time for a couple of murders if it didn't. Or, more likely, one murder. He would not have pressed his luck, Masters reasoned. If his theory of the air-conditioners was in order, Richmond would have murdered Larry Connor first. Later, some time after 3:30, he would have got around to Lila. What Masters really wanted was the name and address of the nurse who had been on duty in the ward during the night-to-morning shift. Without committing himself excessively to the truth, he managed to get both from the desk. The nurse's name was Agnes Morrow. Her address was a small apartment building a few blocks from the hospital.

Masters parked at the curb about fifty feet down the block from the apartment house. By his watch it was after one o'clock—past his lunch time, but Masters was not hungry; besides, he was as usual on a diet. Assuming that Nurse Morrow, off duty at 7:00 A.M., had sacked up by 8:00, she had been sleeping for over five hours. Five hours' sleep was enough for Masters, who did not sleep well, but it probably wasn't for Agnes Morrow, who probably did. He decided to take a chance nevertheless, and he got out of his car. In the lobby directory he located Agnes Morrow's apartment number and went up and rang her bell.

He was in luck. Nurse Morrow was up, though not dressed. That is, she was in pajamas and a terry-cloth robe. Masters, however, was not stimulated by the proximity of this intimate attire. Agnes Morrow had maintained a single estate for over forty years and gave the depressing impression of having maintained her chastity through every day of them. Lean-and-going-gray-and-no-nonsense-about-her. She looked as if she would speak tersely and directly, just shy of barking; he was right.

"Yes?"

"Miss Agnes Morrow?"

"That's right."

"My name is Masters. Lieutenant. Police. I'd like to talk to you. Confidential matter." The terseness and directness of his own speech was an automatic reaction to hers. Masters had the flexibility of a chameleon, or an actor; it was one of his assets in his work.

"Come in."

Masters sat on the edge of a gray sofa while Miss Morrow claimed an uncomfortable high-backed armchair. She sat with her back parallel to, but not touching, the back of the chair; and she gripped the arms as if prepared to jump to her feet at the first threat to her virginity.

"I was told at the hospital," Masters said, "that you've been working the eleven P.M. to seven A.M. shift."

"I have."

"You were on duty as usual on the night of Saturday-Sunday just past?"

"Of course. I haven't missed a tour of duty for fifteen years."

"You had, I believe, an obstetrics case during that night?"

"We had two OB's."

"I'm referring to the one in which Dr. Jack Richmond was the attending physician."

"Oh, yes. Labor was slower than seemed indicated when Dr. Richmond was called. He had to wait around in the hospital about two hours."

"He was there two hours and ten minutes, according to the desk."

"I didn't hold a watch on him."

"That's what I want to talk to you about. Are you sure Dr. Richmond was there *all* the time?"

"Certainly."

"Did you have him constantly under observation?"

"Of course not. I'm far too busy to watch anyone constantly."

"But you said you were sure he was there all the time."

"I said I was sure. I didn't say I could prove it. When Dr. Richmond saw he had to wait for the birth, he asked if there was a bed available so he could lie down. There was an empty private room at the end of the hall, and I saw him go into it. He was there an hour or so later when I went to get him. There is absolutely no reason for me to think he left the room in the interim."

"He went directly to the room when you told him it was available?"

"First he called his wife and told her he would be delayed at the hospital. Then he went to the room."

"You say the private room is at the end of the hall. Is there a stairway at that end?"

"That is correct."

"Does the stairway go down to an outside exit?"

"Yes. The door is locked at night, but it can be opened from inside."

"Can the lock be set so the door will open from the outside?"

"Not without a key."

But, thought Masters, it could be left ajar. A stick, a folded piece of paper—anything inserted between door and jamb—would do the trick.

"So Dr. Richmond wasn't seen between the time he entered the room and the time you notified him his patient was ready?"

"I didn't actually *see* him, no."

"Did anyone else on duty?"

"I have no idea. See here," snapped Nurse Morrow. "Why are you asking me all these questions about Dr. Richmond? I don't make it a practice to discuss doctors."

"Of course you don't," said Masters soothingly. "But this is a police matter, Miss Morrow—"

"What police matter? I have a right to know why I'm being questioned!"

"The evening paper should tell you all about it. Two deaths are involved, at least one of which is a murder, and it's my job to check out people who knew the deceased. Dr. Richmond was one of their friends—there are no professional considerations involved at all." Masters smiled. "All right, Miss Morrow?"

The nurse said slowly, "I see."

"Then could I ask you to inquire around among the other personnel on duty that night—I mean about whether Dr. Richmond was seen leaving that private room at any time between his entering it and your summoning him to his patient?"

She was silent. Then she said, "All right, Lieutenant Masters." She rose. "Now if you'll excuse me—"

"Thanks. Let me know if you turn up anything."

Masters left quickly. A tough cookie, he thought. Naturally close-mouthed about the affairs of the doctors she had to work with, but undoubtedly conscientious and with a rigid code that would cut, when necessary, across professional lines. He had no doubt that she would report to him if she discovered anything.

He drove over to headquarters, where he went to his desk. The coroner's report, relayed from the coroner's physician who had performed the autopsies, placed the time of Lila Connor's death between, roughly, midnight Saturday and 3:00 A.M. Sunday. Larry Connor's death was estimated to have occurred considerably later, between 5:00 and 8:00 A.M. Sunday. It gave a picture of a wife-killer having trouble making up his mind to take his own life, too. Had he actually, after stabbing Lila, sat alone in his office for so long, trying to nerve himself to committing suicide—regretting, perhaps, the shambles of his life? It was possible. A man about to kill himself is not necessarily in a hurry to get it done.

Masters wondered if he weren't flogging a dead man. After all, it had seemed a virtual certainty from the beginning that Larry Connor had killed his wife and then himself. All the circumstantial evidence pointed to it; now it had strong support in the post-mortems. On the other hand, what did he, Masters, have to pit against it? The thinnest kind of theorizing, without a fact to bolster it. Two turned-off air-conditioners. A missing back-door key—that may have been lost or mislaid or could otherwise be accounted for. A cerebral leap in the dark made him wonder if someone might not have killed Larry Connor in his office and then slipped over to the Connor house with Larry's key to kill Lila Connor.

Masters sat at his desk and sucked his thumb, staring into cerebral space.

For someone to have so manipulated conditions as to produce the medical finding that Larry Connor had died appreciably later than Lila Connor—when, according to Masters's theory, he had actually died before—it would have been necessary, ideally, for the manipulator to do two things: He had secretly to speed up the process of organic decay in Lila's corpse and slow it down in Larry's. To accelerate decomposition in the wife's body meant turning *off* the air-conditioning in the Connor house; to retard decomposition in the husband's body meant turning the air-conditioning *on* in his office. But for the deception to be completely successful, the killer had to do two subsequent things: Return to the Connor house and turn the house air-conditioning back *on,* so that when Lila's body was found *it would be assumed that the air-conditioner had been on uninterruptedly from the moment of death;* and return to Larry Connor's office and turn the office air-conditioner *off,* so that when Connor's body was found *it would be assumed that the air-conditioning had been off uninterruptedly from the moment of death.*

With such false assumptions the medical conclusions were bound to be false. The far more advanced decomposition of Lila's body must produce the finding that Lila had been dead a longer time than was actually the case; the less advanced decomposition of Larry's body must produce the finding that Larry had been dead a shorter time than was actually the case.

That is, thought Masters wryly, if I'm not pipe dreaming.

Even the pipe dream, he thought, had a serious hole in it. For the fact was, the killer had *not* returned to the Connor house, long after killing Lila, to turn the house air-conditioner back on, even though—assuming there was any validity to the theory at all—he *had* returned to the Connor office to turn the office air-conditioner off.

Did the failure to get back into the Connor house invalidate the theory? Not necessarily. The fact was, even with the house air-conditioner *known* to have been off since the time of Lila's death, the medical finding placed her death first; in other words, as it turned out, the deception was successful merely through the manipulation of the office air-conditioner and its effect in retarding the decomposition of Larry's body. It may well have been, Masters thought, that the killer found no opportunity to get back into the Connor house to turn the air-conditioner on. The houses were fairly well clustered together; the immediate neighbors were all friends; going back without being seen entering or leaving may simply have been too dangerous. The situation was different in the case of the Connor office; it was in the business district, the day was a Sunday when all offices and stores were closed, and entry to the Connor office could be gained through the entirely unobserved alley door at the rear.

Masters felt his head to steady it. How had he got himself into this thought-maze?

Another logical question: If the killer had to return to Larry Connor's office to turn off the air-conditioner, why at the same time hadn't he restored to Larry's key-case the key to the back door of the Connor residence, which he had had to borrow at the time he killed Larry in order to get into the Connor house and kill Lila? The fact was, the killer had *not* restored the key to Larry's key-case on his return visit to the office. Did *this* fact invalidate the whole theory?

Not necessarily again. Perhaps it had simply slipped the killer's mind in the extreme tension of his murderous activities. Or it had not occurred to him that the local police, with their relative inexperience of murder cases, would notice that the key was missing—or, if they did notice, would attach any significance to it.

And also, maybe the country cop would be just observant and smart enough to make a horse's patoot out of himself!

Masters sighed and shut his eyes and rocked back in his swivel-chair. To quit or go ahead, that was the question.

He began to review the case in his mind. In the chronological order of the review, he was standing again in Larry Connor's office, having just entered it, and he was seeing Larry Connor stretched out on the sofa, right hand trailing on the floor. There for some reason the scene became fixed, like a stopped film. Masters continued to study it.

After a long time he reached for the report he had found on his desk early that morning. He read it again, carefully.

"Oh!" he said. "Oh, by God!"

From his desk drawer he took a telephone directory and frantically searched for a number.

11

"Oh!" said Nancy. "Oh, by God!"

She was not aware that this was an echo of Lieutenant Masters, several hours delayed; and neither, of course, was David. They were sprawled on their terrace, David trying to finish reading a chapter in the fading light, which was something Nancy had told him and told him not to do. He looked up, startled.

"What's the matter?"

"I have just this minute thought of something," said Nancy.

"Thought of what?"

"It's just *incredible*."

"In that case don't tell me."

"I mean it's incredible that I haven't thought of it before."

David was properly titillated. "Oh? Yes? Well?"

"Because it was obvious to anyone with half a brain, and it has been all along."

"Damn it, will you kindly tell me what you're talking about?"

"Why, the light."

"Well, you may see the light, but I'm completely in the dark."

"That's because you weren't outside the house, as I was."

"When?"

"The night Lila was killed. You remember I talked

100

with Larry out front and later with Stanley out back, and some time during that period I saw the light on in Lila's bedroom? I definitely remember seeing it. Well, the next day, when you and Jack and I went up and found Lila dead in the bedroom, *no light was burning*. Don't you see what it means, David? *It means that Lila must have been alive after Larry left!* Dead people can't turn off lights!"

The chapter would clearly remain unfinished. David dogeared a page to mark his place and closed the book.

"You're sure Lila's light was on *after* Larry drove off?"

"I'm *positive*."

"Hmm!" David cogitated. Nancy waited anxiously for his verdict. After all, the man *was* her lord and master. David's face smoothed. "No mystery," he said cheerfully. "The bulb burned out."

"Darn, that didn't occur to me." Nancy brightened. "But we can check that. Let's run over there and look at the bulb."

"We can't, dear heart. Remember? House locked? Police?"

Nancy was silent. Then she said, "The police do have a talent for getting in the way, don't they? I suppose I'll have to call Lieutenant Masters to open the house. Don't you agree, David?"

"To anything," said David cravenly, "as long as you leave me out of it. Anyway, it occurs to me that the answer to the doused bedroom light may be very simple. Larry may have come back later and turned it off."

"No," said Nancy firmly.

"Why not?"

"Because."

"Because why?"

"Just because."

"Oh." David squirmed uneasily. "Damn it, I'm not fond of any of this! It makes Masters's nonsense suddenly seem to make sense. That stuff he told you today. Do you suppose he can be right? That one of our neighbors is a murderer?"

"I don't know . . . It makes me feel like a kind of traitor . . . Anyway, aside from who—*why?*"

"There could have been an unknown reason."

Nancy sniffed. "In a neighborhood like this *everything* is known."

"Is it?" asked David dryly. "Did you know, for instance, that Lila and Jack Richmond had a thing going for a while?"

"Oh, come off it, David!"

"It's a fact. It lasted for about six months. Jack broke it off."

"Dave Howell," exclaimed Nancy, "I simply can't believe that something like that went on right under our noses without my knowing it!"

"It didn't go on right under our noses. It went on at a considerable distance from our noses. They were careful to see to *that.*"

"Then how do you know so much about it?"

"I don't. I know only the little Jack chose to confide in me. We were at the club drinking, and it suddenly spilled out. I think Jack was in need of a confessor. I gathered the thing got pretty torrid before it cooled off."

"Isn't that just-like a man? Has an affair with his neighbor's wife and blabs about it in a bar! That Jack is far too handsome for his own good, if you ask me. Why the hell didn't you tell me about this before?"

"All men don't blab," said David loftily.

"You're blabbing now, aren't you?"

"This is different. We were trying to think of a possible motive for a neighbor. I just cited it as a theoretical possibility—"

"David Howell, how can you play golf and drink beer with someone you suspect of murder?"

"Damn it, I *don't* suspect Jack! Of course it's ridiculous."

"You may think it's ridiculous, but I can assure you Lieutenant Masters wouldn't. That man could suspect anyone, including you and me. Did Larry know about this thing between Jack and Lila?"

"I doubt it. I never noticed any change in his attitude toward Jack."

"Did Vera?"

"Jack didn't actually say, but I suspect she did. Vera's pretty sharp. She'd be hard to two-time indefinitely, and I rather imagine this wasn't the first time Jack grazed in another pasture."

"Do you have to express it so disgustingly?" Nancy asked absently, but her mind was busy with the problem. "If Vera knew, she certainly didn't let on. She always treated Lila quite well—well enough to fool *me*, if she knew about Lila and Jack. Treated Lila well and didn't like her, all at the same time."

"Well, Vera's a remarkable gal. Even if she found out about Jack and Lila, she'd be quite capable of adjusting —once Jack had got out of the affair."

"This isn't getting us anywhere," Nancy decided. "David. Do you know who sticks in my mind? I mean as a possible murderer?"

"Me?"

"Besides you."

"I give up."

"Stanley."

"Old *Stanley*?"

"Yes, old Stanley."

"That's just downright idiotic."

"Is it? I keep remembering that Stanley remained in the alley when I went into the house. I happened to glance back, and he was staring up at Lila's lighted window in the most peculiar way. How seriously, I wonder, did he take Lila's passes? She only tried to tease him, of course—a kind of ridicule—but Stanley has no sense at all where women are concerned. On top of that, he's thin-skinned. I wonder what he'd do if, after being teased into a compromising act, he found himself laughed at and made to feel a fool?"

"I certainly can't see Stanley going berserk with a knife under *any* provocation."

"Can't you? Men are so obtuse about such things."

"But it wasn't only Lila who was killed. By Masters's theory, so was Larry. Are you seriously contending that old Stanley, after stabbing Lila in a rage, was capable of devising an elaborate scheme to kill Larry and make him seem a murderer-suicide? Even if Stanley had the time that night, he lacks the imagination. The fact is, lovey, I'm not convinced Larry was killed by anyone but himself. I think he committed suicide, as the evidence indicates."

"Wouldn't that be accommodating of him! Quite a coincidence! Larry killed himself just in time to be blamed for the murder of Lila, who was really murdered by Stanley. No, *thank* you."

"We have three theories," said David. "Murder and suicide by Larry. Or two murders by a party unknown. Or a suicide and a coincidental murder by a party unknown. Well, regardless of lights and keys and air-conditioners and whatever Masters can make of them, I still plump for Number One. It's too bad, but it's simple and indicated, and that's enough for me."

"And that light in Lila's room?" demanded Nancy. "It had to be turned off by *someone*, if it didn't burn out."

"Maybe Stanley turned it off."

"Speaking of Stanley, here he comes."

Stanley Walters had been in his backyard watching them furtively for some time. Now he came down to the alley and crossed it and waddled up to the Howells' terrace. He looked nervous and worried and not at all like a scheming killer, let alone a principal in a crime of passion.

"Hello, Stanley," David said.

"Hello, Stanley," Nancy said. "How's Mae?"

"Mae's not so well," Stanley said. "She's lying down. Headache."

"Oh," Nancy said. "Will you have a beer or something?"

"No, thanks." Stanley sat down and clasped his hands and inspected them as if for stains. Then he closed his knees upon them. "I'd . . . like to talk to you folks. I mean there's something on my mind that I can't, well, get off it."

"Telling somebody about it," said Nancy warmly, "is the best kind of therapy, Stanley. Thanks for thinking of us as confidants."

"Yes," said David. "What's on your mind, old boy?"

"It happened the night Lila was killed." Stanley looked up toward the bedroom window of the house next door; he kept looking at it as he went on. "I know Larry is supposed to have killed Lila before he left home. It isn't true. Because I was over there *after* he left, and Lila was still alive."

"You *saw* Lila?" Nancy cried. "See, David?"

"He didn't say he saw Lila," said David. "He said she was still alive."

"Of course he saw her! How else would he know whether she was alive or not?"

"Because he could have just heard her voice."

"That's ridiculous. Stanley, you did see Lila, didn't you?"

"Yes. I saw her and talked with her," Stanley said miserably. "And I don't mind telling you I wish to hell I hadn't."

"There, David, I hope you're satisfied. Now stop in-interrupting, will you? Go on, Stanley. Why did you go over to Lila's?"

It was apparent from Stanley's instant flush that this was the $64,000 question. It was also apparent—from his tone of voice—that on this particular point his need for unburdening his soul was not so great as to demand the entirely naked truth.

"Well . . . I was down there at the alley, see . . . as you know, Nancy . . . and I couldn't help, well, thinking about Lila—I mean, kind of worrying and wondering if she was all right, being all alone in the house and all—so I finally went over to find out."

You finally went over to try to earn a few extramarital credits, David thought; but he did not vocalize it.

"You actually went into the house?" Nancy asked, with a sharp look at her husband. That woman, David thought, is a telepath.

"Nnnno . . . she wouldn't let me in. I mean, Lila seemed to think I was coming over for, well, ulterior reasons." Stanley began to sweat. He took out a handkerchief and blotted himself.

"And exactly what happened, Stanley? This could be *very* important. Don't leave out a *thing*. Well?"

"Well, I went over there to the back door and rang the bell, and Lila opened her bedroom window upstairs and poked her head out and asked me what the devil I wanted. I told her I just wanted to see if she was all right. She laughed and said something like, 'No sale tonight, buster,' and told me to go away, so I did." Stanley had to blot again. "And that's it. There wouldn't have been that much if I'd had the sense I was born with."

"You say she opened her window?" Nancy muttered. "Did she shut it again?"

"Yes, Nancy."

Nancy whirled on David. "Jack told Lieutenant Masters that Lila and Larry were probably going to open windows, to explain why we found the air-conditioning turned off. Jack said they probably just didn't get to it. That's not true, obviously, because Lila opened the window to Stanley *and then closed it again*. Why didn't she simply leave it open if the air-conditioning was already off?"

"She may have closed it without thinking," David said. "You know? Habit?"

"Think that if you choose," Nancy said coldly. "I don't."

.. "Anyway," said Stanley, "that's what I've had on my mind. I'm wondering what to do about it."

"That's no problem, Stanley," Nancy said. "You must tell Lieutenant Masters. It's your civic duty."

"I suppose I must." Stanley glanced uneasily in the direction of his house. "I was hoping I wouldn't have to. Mae will never believe I just went over to see if Lila was all right."

"As for that," Nancy said cheerily, "I'm not so sure I believe it myself. However! The police are discreet about such matters, Stanley. They won't tell Mae unless it's absolutely necessary."

"Just the same," mumbled Stanley, "I wish I didn't have to tell them at all."

"Would you like me to tell Lieutenant Masters for you? I have to talk to him in the morning, anyhow—"

"Would you, Nancy?" Stanley looked abjectly grateful. "Thanks! Not that it will help much, I guess. Lieutenant Masters will probably be around to talk to me anyway."

"That," David said, "is as sure as zeroes in September."

Stanley sighed; he seemed for an appalling moment to be on the verge of tears. Then, without another word, he trudged back across the alley and through the backyard to his house.

"Poor old Stanley," David said. "Why do you suppose he confessed?"

"Because he thought he might be found out," Nancy said. "It's often smart tactics to volunteer a story before it's flung in your teeth. That way you establish a reputation for truth. So you can lie about or leave out something damaging and maybe get away with it."

"Darned," exclaimed her husband, "if you aren't getting to sound more like Masters every minute!"

"That," said Nancy, "is because I'm beginning to *think* like him."

12

There were several things that Lieutenant Masters had to do at headquarters the next morning, the foremost of which was to convince his chief that further investigation of the Connor case was justified. More, that it was mandatory; and Masters said so as clearly as he could.

"Are you sure, Gus?" the chief said. "By God, you'd better be."

"I'm sure," Masters said. "I'd be tickled to death to drop the case if I weren't."

"But you have to have something to base it on. And don't bother to tell me again about the air-conditioners and the key that's missing. Accentuate the positive."

"Well, there's something I got onto yesterday. It almost got past me, it was so obvious."

"Well, well?"

"It's evidence that Lila Connor was murdered by someone *not* her husband, who probably murdered her husband, too."

"There you go again! Damn it, if ever there was a case that seemed closed as soon as it opened, this was it! All right, Gus. What's this evidence you're talking about?"

"Yesterday afternoon I was sitting here wondering whether to go on or give the case up, and all of a sudden I remembered something I'd seen in Connor's office. I remembered seeing him lying on the sofa there, his right arm dangling over the side. He was in his shirt sleeves, and on his wrist below the edge of the cuff was a watch. *On his right wrist.* It's not incontrovertible, but it strongly indicated that Larry Connor must have been left-handed. So I called his secretary, Ruth Benton, for verification, and I was right. Connor *was* left-handed."

"So what?"

"The fingerprint report established that Larry Connor's prints—and his only—were on the handle of the murder weapon. *The prints of his right hand.* But he was left-handed! Don't you see what that means?" In his enthusiasm Masters poked the chief's collarbone with his forefinger, which was as horny as a dragon's claw, and the chief recoiled. "It means, Chief, that those prints of Connor's *were planted on that letter-opener* by someone who hadn't noticed or didn't know or simply forgot that Connor was left-handed! Which logically means that they were planted *after Connor died,* in his office! Which means the murder weapon was only *then* taken to the Connor house to kill Lila Connor with! Which means the husband couldn't have murdered her! And if he didn't murder her, why would he commit suicide?"

"Wait, wait," the chief groaned, holding his head. "Can you prove the letter-opener was taken from the office to the house?"

"It *follows,* Chief."

"So does my dog a bitch in heat," said the chief coarsely, "but it doesn't mean he gets it."

"Chief," said Masters. "Ruth Benton, Connor's secretary, will settle this—she's coming in this morning to look at the letter-opener. She says it sounds like the one Connor kept on his office desk, but she'll be able to say definitely when she sees it."

The chief, rocking like an old lady, cursed softly. He obviously foresaw bad times.

"You win, Gus. Go ahead with it. But I'm not authorizing any three-month la-de-da. How long do you figure you need?"

Masters thought rapidly. He figured it would take a week. "Ten days," he said.

"I'll give you a week. Any idea who's getting the nose-ring?"

"Not yet."

"You're lying. All right, go to it." As Masters turned to leave, the chief said, "When you do pull the pinch, you better be sure."

"Sure, Chief."

"*Damn* sure," the chief said grimly.

The detective went back to his office. On the way he noted that the clock in the hall stood at a few minutes past nine. Ruth Benton had agreed to come in at nine-thirty.

In the meantime there were a few other items on his agenda. Lila Connor's second husband, he recalled, was said to have been a suicide. If so, there would be a police record; and Masters called Kansas City headquarters and asked for it and any other information pertinent. The police report alone, however, wasn't likely to contain the kind of material he was after. He put through a second call, to a private K.C. agency, and commissioned a quick investigation, supplying as many leads as he could in order to expedite matters. Whereupon Masters sat back to wait for Ruth Benton, with fifteen minutes to go. Only three of them had passed when his phone rang. He recognized the voice at the first word. What a voice!

"This is Nancy Howell speaking," the voice said. Temple bells, pure temple bells.

"Oh, hello, Mrs. Howell. I didn't expect to hear from you again."

"Because of yesterday, you mean?"

"Yes. I definitely got the impression that I was off your calling list."

"Well, something's come up that changes things. Would you like to hear what it is?"

"Very much. Why don't you come downtown and tell me?"

"It would be better if you came up here. There's something I want to do that I need your help for. It's a —well, an experiment."

"Can you be a little more definite?"

"I'd rather not. All I will say now is that we must get into the Connor house to do it."

"The Connor house? You bet, Mrs. Howell! See you soon."

He had just hung up when Ruth Benton, a few minutes early, arrived. Masters saw at once that Ruth Benton had been having a bad time. A secretary did not develop such bags under her eyes through sorrow over a mere kindly employer.

"Thank you for coming in, Miss Benton," Masters said. "This will only take a minute. As I told you over the phone, I want you to look at the weapon used to kill Mrs. Connor."

He had the lethal letter-opener in a paper-lined box on his desk. He removed the lid, revealing the blood-caked weapon. Ruth Benton closed her eyes, then opened them again.

"Yes," she said. "That's Larry's letter-opener. He always kept it on his office desk."

"Are you sure?"

"Positive."

"Would you be willing to testify under oath to that effect?"

"I suppose so, but why? Does it mean that Larry didn't kill his wife, or that he did?"

"It may prove that he didn't."

"Then who did?"

Masters rose. "Thanks for coming in, Miss Benton."

The girl rose, too, accepting her dismissal with a

shrug. "If Larry was guilty, I don't blame him. If he was innocent, I'll do anything I can to help prove it."

In Shady Acres, Masters parked before the Howell house and went around to the back door. He found Nancy Howell, adorable in a crisp lavender housedress, pulling the stems from strawberries, which gave her hands the rather startling illusion that she had been dipping them in fresh blood. He entered, hat in hand, humbly, to be invited to sit at her kitchen table. Her offer of coffee thrilled him to the bone. It meant that he had been paroled, if not pardoned outright.

"Sorry I was held up, Mrs. Howell—oh, thank you," said Masters, accepting the coffee. "I hope I didn't keep you waiting?"

"That's all right, Lieutenant," said Nancy, "there's no rush. Actually, I've decided I owe you an apology. One never feels in any particular hurry to apologize to someone, does one?"

"As far as I am concerned, Mrs. Howell, go no further. You owe me nothing. Certainly no apology."

"Why, thank you, Lieutenant. That's very generous of you."

Masters sipped his coffee. He really wanted cream and sugar, but he was afraid to ask for them. The coffee was also bitter, from having been standing on the range for God knew how long. Nevertheless, he sipped it with every appearance of relish.

"Well!" said Masters. "Now what about this experiment of yours, Mrs. Howell? You said something about getting into the Connor house?"

"You carry a key to the house, don't you? I want you to take me inside."

"Why do you want to go inside?"

"I want to try the light in Lila's bedroom. To see if it will go on."

Masters blinked. "I don't suppose you'd mind explaining?"

"I happened to remember that on the night Lila was killed the light in her bedroom was on—I mean after Larry left. I definitely recall seeing it. But the next day, when we found Lila's body, the light was *off*."

"You don't say." Masters regarded her with admiration and respect. This might prove an important confirmation of part of his theory. "You're assuming that the light was turned off by Lila?"

"Or by somebody else. In either event, it shows that somebody was in that house after Larry left—and that ought to go a long way toward clearing Larry's name."

"Unless, of course, the bulb simply burned out."

"Of course. That's why I want to examine the bulb."

"It won't be necessary, Mrs. Howell. The bulb was not burned out. We've had it on since then."

"The bedlight, too?"

"Bedlight? No . . . Could it have been the bedlight you saw?"

"I doubt it. But there's no sense in leaving any possibility unexplored, is there, Lieutenant?"

"You're right there! Let's go over and settle the matter, shall we?"

They entered the Connor house by the front door and went directly upstairs to Lila's bedroom. Masters, preceding her into the room, stepped aside.

"It was your idea, Mrs. Howell," he said archly. "You try them."

The room was full of shadows, and Nancy moved reluctantly through them to the hapless double bed. The bedlight came on readily. She turned it off again just as Masters flipped the wall-switch that operated the ceiling fixture.

"That settles it," Nancy said. "No burned-out bulb, and it was definitely the ceiling light I saw. The bedlight casts most of its light on the bed, and anyway it's much less bright."

"You've established an important point." Masters looked around. "By the way, as long as we're here, there's something else I want to look for. Do you mind waiting?"

"What is it you're after, Lieutenant?"

"A key. A key to the back door. We found Lila's in the key-case in her purse, so hers is accounted for. But her husband's is missing."

"What grisly fun," Nancy said. "Do you mind if I help you look for it, Lieutenant? I'm not much good at standing around waiting. I get itches in all the inconvenient places."

"Well," Masters said doubtfully. "It's against the rules—"

"Whose rules—that doddering old police chief's?" Nancy said with scorn. "Or—" and Masters flinched under the beautiful fire that leaped into her eyes—"or am I still a suspect, Lieutenant Masters?"

"No, no, no," he said hastily. "By all means help me look!"

For the better part of an hour they worked their way through the house, searching every place they could think of where a key might have been left or lost or hidden. But they failed to find it. At last they came back to the room in which they had begun; and Nancy, conceding defeat, sat down on the edge of Lila's elegant chaise. But Masters went once more around the room, and then disappeared in the bathroom. When he came out he was looking rather inscrutable.

"If you ask me," Nancy said, "this is a waste of time. I told you the back door was unlocked when I tried it Sunday afternoon. I don't see why you persist in thinking that it was locked before."

"Is it reasonable that the Connors left their back door unlocked? Even at night?"

"No, but they may have neglected to lock it that particular night. After all, they'd been drinking a lot of beer and quarreling. A drinkie-fightie episode can make married people forget to take their shoes off when they go to bed, let alone a little thing like locking the back door."

"No, the murderer couldn't have counted on that, Mrs. Howell. He would still have had to bring the back-door key with him, in case the door *was* locked."

"Then maybe he still has it."

"That would make him out an idiot," said Masters, "and, whoever it is we're dealing with, he's certainly no idiot."

"Or just threw it away."

"Maybe." Masters sounded cryptic.

"Lieutenant, you know something!" Nancy was so excited that she grabbed Master's arm, leaning very close to him. Masters closed his eyes momentarily; her perfume made him feel faint. "Come on, what is it? Tell me!"

"Well, I do have an idea," he said weakly.

"What?"

"I'd rather not say now. It may be all wet."

This clearly closed the subject, so Nancy let Masters walk her back to her house. On the terrace he lifted his hat and was about to depart when Nancy said, "Oh, I almost forgot!" and detained him a little longer, belatedly recalling Stanley Walters's confession about having talked to Lila that night after Nancy went back into her house. Masters listened with mounting bitterness, glaring at the alley where Stanley had been standing on the night under discussion.

"That settles it," the detective growled when Nancy had finished. "Why didn't Walters himself tell me this?"

"Don't blame Stanley too much, Lieutenant," Nancy said. "He's in mortal terror of his wife. Mae can be very unpleasant where other women are concerned."

Recalling Mae Walters, Masters did not doubt it. Just the same, he was boiling mad.

"Walters should have told me," he said. "It's a serious offense withholding evidence in a murder investigation. It's cost me a lot of time and headaches. I could have got off to a flying start on this case, instead of floundering around in the swamp of my own thick head!"

"Stanley didn't withhold it," Nancy said quickly, a little frightened by this unexpected side to Lieutenant Masters. "He was just a little late in giving it, Lieutenant. He actually asked me to tell you."

Masters grunted. "I'll deal with Mr. Walters later. The point is, the evidence is now conclusive. Lila Connor was definitely alive after you saw Larry Connor leave home, and that practically puts the clincher on the conclusion that he didn't kill her, and consequently didn't commit suicide, either. Walters's testimony fits with other evidence I have. As far as I'm concerned, there's no doubt now that we're dealing with a live murderer of two people; and unless I'm going soft in the head, he's living somewhere around here."

And Masters stalked off toward his car.

13

There was a man coming down the alley, trying doors.
If the rear of a building was flush with the alley, he
would pause merely long enough to assure himself that
the back door was secured; but if there was a parking
area between the building and the alley, he disappeared
for a minute or two and Masters knew he was trying
another door out of the line of sight. The door-tester
dragged one leg, the result of an injury years ago when
he was a brakeman on the railroad. He had received a
large settlement at the time; but the money was long
gone, and now he lived on a small pension supple-
mented by his earnings as a night watchman. His name
was Jake Kimble.

Masters, waiting on a side street at the end of the
alley, could follow Jake's progress by the approaching
flashlight; he could also hear the slithering sound of
Jake's maimed foot dragging over the uneven brick. The
detective was familiar with old Kimble's route. He had
been waiting now for a quarter of an hour. It had occurred to Masters that the watchman might be the pos-
sessor of vital information.

In due course Jake Kimble emerged from the darkness into the glow of the street lamp.

"Hello, Jake," Masters said.

"Hello?" The old man was startled. He peered
through the poor light. "Lieutenant Masters?"

"That's right. Any trouble, Jake?"

"No. No trouble."

"You had a little trouble the other night, though, didn't you?"

"Not me, Lieutenant," old Jake said quickly.

Masters laughed. "Wouldn't you call a suicide unusual?"

"Oh, you mean Mr. Connor killing himself in his office after killing his wife. No, he didn't make any trouble. Not for me, anyway."

"Saturday night, wasn't it?"

"Saturday night my first round. Sunday morning when I came round again."

"Did you try his back door both times?"

"Yes, *sir*. And it was locked. I know my job, Lieutenant."

"I know you do, Jake. I'm on the case, and I wondered if you noticed anything special."

"Can't say I did. He wasn't in his office on my first round, I'm sure of that. But he was there, all right, when I came round again. Maybe already dead."

"How do you know?"

"That he was dead? I don't. I said maybe."

"Not that he was dead. That he was there."

"Why, his car was parked behind the building!"

Masters smiled ruefully to himself. "Any other reason?"

"Sure. He's got an air-conditioner stuck in the window next to the back door. First time around it wasn't running. The second time it was."

It was a little after eleven. Having shot so much of the evening, Masters decided he might as well shoot a little more. He left town by the main highway; and fifteen minutes later, halfway to Kansas City, he parked before a fancy building decorated with stone urns and glass brick and a giant's intestine of neon tubing.

There was an elegantly carpeted lobby, and beyond it

a large room crowded with tables, which he surveyed from the entrance. Not all the tables were occupied; week-night business was relatively slow. At the moment the room was dark except for a bright bluish spotlight, in which a girl in a tight evening gown was singing to the accompaniment of a small combo. Inside the entrance, armed with a stack of menus, stood a maître-d' in a tux that was only slightly bluer than his jowls. This man surveyed Masters coldly. Well, Masters conceded, he surely didn't look like much in his crumpled suit and wilted shirt and tired tie.

"A table for one . . . sir?" The "sir" was grudging.

"No," Masters said. "I'm looking."

"For a friend? Maybe I can help you."

"I wouldn't call him a friend. Lewis Shrill. Is he here?"

"Mr. Shrill is in his office, but I don't think he can be disturbed."

"We'll disturb each other." He flipped open his badge case. "Don't bother, friend. I know the way."

The office was to the left, behind a heavy oak door. Masters knocked, and a voice that seemed to come past a large obstruction told him to come in. Masters went in.

The obstruction was composed of scrambled eggs and chicken livers. Lewis Shrill was eating his supper. It reminded Masters that it had been a long time since dinner and it would be a longer time until breakfast. He helped himself to a chair by Shrill's desk.

"Have a chair, Gus," Shrill said.

Masters parked his hat on the floor beside him. "Don't let me interrupt your supper, Lew."

"You want some? I'll order another plate and fork."

"I'd better pass. Someone might see me and think it was a pay-off."

"Still satisfied with peanuts, hey, Gus? If there's one thing that gripes me more than a crooked cop, it's an honest one."

"I came for a favor," Masters said, smiling.

"You're outside your jurisdiction, ain't you?"

"Outside my jurisdiction, out of my element, and maybe out of line."

Shrill stopped shoveling it in long enough to stare at Masters. Then he said, "You tell me what it is, we'll see."

He went back to his eggs and livers, and Masters watched him with a watering mouth. It was certainly coincidence, but Shrill's voice—even clogged with food—was compatible with his name. High, lilting, almost effeminate. Coming from that gross body, it was ludicrous. Until you learned, or were taught, that there was nothing ludicrous about the man whatever. Shrill had a vast dark face with little still eyes imbedded in darker puffs of flesh; his hair, parted in the middle, was as black and shiny as a toupee, which it was. He also possessed an effeminate hunger for gossip, preferably of a sexual nature. Shrill knew more disreputable things about more unlikely people than anyone in the Middle West. To raid this storehouse of information was the purpose of Masters's visit.

"I'm after information, Lew," Masters said.

"Since when do the cops have to come to me for information?"

"You're a short cut, and I'm running out of time."

"Get to it, Gus. What do you want?" Shrill kept eating with a steady voracity.

"Anything you can give me on two people. Lila Connor and Dr. Jack Richmond."

Shrill's fork halted in mid-air. After a moment, it finished its trip and returned to the plate. Shrill's jaws worked. His voice made its way through what his jaws were working on.

"The lady's dead, Gus. I don't talk about dead people. It's bad luck."

"Take a chance this time, Lew. I need this."

"You night-flying or something? Doing divorce work on the side?"

"So it was grounds for divorce," grinned Masters.

"Don't play tag with me, Gus. It was also grounds for murder, from what I read. Her husband knocked her off, and I wouldn't have been surprised except he wasn't exactly lily-white and clean-o himself."

"You mean a certain secretary?"

"Oh, you know about Connor and her." Lewis Shrill seemed surprised. Suddenly he laughed. "Hell, it's no skin off my nose. You want to know about the doc? Well, he likes variety. The Connor broad wasn't his first, and she won't be the last."

"Lew." Masters leaned forward. "What's the dirt on Richmond and the Connor woman? Was he way in over his head with her?"

The fat man shrugged. "Who the hell knows a thing like that? He gave her a long play, that I do know. He even brought her here a few times—that's what made me curious. I get my kicks out of guys like the doc, and sometimes—you know, Gus—I can turn an honest dollar out of what I find. I've got connections in K.C.—hotels, motels, private agencies, you know? I arranged to get some reports."

"And?"

Shrill winked. It was startling, like seeing a Buddha wink. "Those reports made spicy reading. I could account for a few nights that Mrs. Doc, say, might like to know about."

"Involving Lila Connor?"

Shrill pushed his plate aside and wiped his lips on a tablecloth-sized napkin. He folded the napkin meticulously and laid it beside the well-shined plate.

"Yeah," he said, "involving Lila Connor, and I'll tell you this, Gus. That guy Richmond was lucky to get out of it so easy. She was a real mean broad—the kind that acts like a nympho and she ain't even breathing hard."

Masters stooped and retrieved his hat. "Did you turn an honest dollar, Lew, on the basis of those reports?"

"Now, Gus," squeaked Lewis Shrill, and then his great belly was shaken by a belch. "Excuse *me* . . . Would you believe me if I answered no?"

"No," said Masters.

"Then why ask me? But the fact is, I never got around to that file. Connor cost me a lot of honest dollars."

Masters looked skeptical. Nevertheless, he smiled when he said, "Thanks, Lew," and left.

He thought about stopping in at a diner in town for hamburgers and coffee, but he found that his appetite was gone. He compromised on a couple of shots of rye in a back-street bar.

The Howells were gone and the dark house seemed to be breathing in time with a slow, giant pulse. Vera Richmond, lying in bed beside her husband, listened to the breath and counted the pulse; both were her own. She had been lying on her back for a half hour but she could not sleep. She wondered if she would ever be able to sleep again. She would, of course. Sleep, like death, came in its due time, and maybe in the end there was little difference.

"Are you awake?" she said.

"Yes," Jack Richmond said. After a while he said, "I've been thinking."

"So have I. I've been thinking about what Nancy Howell told us tonight. What do you suppose will happen next?"

"I don't know. We may as well face one thing, Vera. Lila was alive after Larry left Saturday night. So either he came back later, or . . . she was killed by somebody else."

They were silent again. After another while, Vera said, "But what about Larry's death? How can you make anything but suicide of that?"

"It's not a question of what I can make of it. It's a question of what the police can make of it. That fellow Masters has demonstrated that he's no fool. God knows what else he's found out or may have in mind."

"It all seemed so simple at first," Vera said. "It would be better if it had stayed that way."

Jack cleared his throat. "All I know is, I can expect a call from Masters any time now. It's bound to come."

"Surely he can't arrest you, Jack! On what evidence?"

"There's no use going over all that again. Motive and opportunity may do me in fine. If Masters can't prove my guilt by direct evidence, neither can I prove my innocence. By the time he's finished he may have a circumstantial case that will sound like proof, even if it isn't."

"It's not fair! I won't let it happen!"

"There's nothing you can do. There's nothing I want you to do. I've been the stupidest kind of jackass, and I suppose I'll have to pay for it. I'm sorry, Vera."

"Everything will come out all right! You'll *see*."

"Yes, dear."

"Jack, can't we move away? I want so much to move to another part of town."

"If it's not too late," Dr. Richmond said.

14

It was later than they thought. It was, in fact, on the next evening that Masters came to see Dr. Jack Richmond. The chances were that it would have been the other way round—Dr. Richmond being called in to see Masters—if Masters had not happened to be in the neighborhood. To be exact, in the house next door.

In the meantime there had been some minor backyard action. Jack had come outside with a trowel and had begun to loosen the dirt around some rose bushes; and David, appearing in his yard a few minutes later, saw Jack at work and decided that he might as well go over and supervise the job. Jack really didn't seem committed to the rose bushes, as indicated by the fact that immediately on spotting David he dropped the trowel and proposed a cold beer on the terrace. David declined feebly as a matter of form. Jack went in to get the beers, which he brought back shortly, and they were there, lolling in canvas chairs, when Nancy came outside looking for her helpmeet.

Expecting him to be at hand, Nancy was slightly aggrieved that he was not. She had been engaged in doing the dinner dishes in her hot kitchen, and it seemed to her that the least she had a right to expect of a husband, if he didn't help, was to stay in his own backyard till the work was done. There he was, however, over on the Richmonds' terrace, swilling beer like a member of the privileged class.

Nancy decided that what was good enough for him was certainly none too good for *her*. She drifted over sweetly and was invited to join them, an unnecessary amenity inasmuch as she had already done so; and when Jack returned with her beer, Vera was with him with a beer of her own.

By unstated agreement they avoided all reference to the Connors, whose remains had been claimed by various out-of-state relatives; and it was a problem to dredge up other topics when there was only one topic in the minds of all.

Jack and Vera, Nancy thought, looked haggard and tense. This was unusual, especially for Vera, who ordinarily adjusted to almost everything without trauma.

The silent house next door cast a shadow and a chill over lawn and hedge and flagstones, and to her annoyance Nancy found herself glancing at it over her shoulder, as if it were ready to spring. Thus it was, glancing back, that she suddenly saw it, and uttered a cry.

"Look!" Nancy said. "There's a light in Lila's room."

"Yes," Vera said. "It came on a few minutes ago."

"Who in the devil could be up there this time of day," David said, "and what in God's name could they be doing?"

"Wait a minute." Jack jumped up and walked around the house. When he returned he grunted, "There's a police car parked out front. It must be that sleuth, Masters."

He sat down again, picked up his can of beer, and leaned back with a deep sigh. It was for all the world as though he could sense the end of something and, sensing it, was relieved.

"What do you suppose he's doing now?" Nancy said thoughtfully. "Could he be looking for the key again?"

"What key?" Jack said.

"The key to the back door. He thinks there was one

in Larry's key-case. Anyway, it's missing. Didn't I tell you?"

"No, you didn't."

"Well, he thinks the murderer may have taken it after killing Larry in order to get into the house afterward and kill Lila."

"Larry committed suicide," Vera said. "Whatever ridiculous notions the police may have, there's no doubt about *that*. If Lila was killed by somebody else, Larry's suicide just happened to occur around the same time."

"That's my opinion too," said David.

"I can tell you," Nancy said, "that that is *not* the opinion of Lieutenant Masters. He made it perfectly clear the other morning when I told him about the light—I mean how it was off after being on at the time Larry left. It was the same morning I told him about Stanley, and how Stanley had seen and talked with Lila after I left him in the alley."

"What are you, a witch or something?" David said. "Every time you mention Stanley, you conjure him up. Here he comes with Mae."

"I think," said Vera, "that I cannot possibly tolerate Mae this evening."

But Vera managed to tolerate Mae after all. The Walterses declined beer and sat down stiffly. It was apparent that their marital relationship was in precariously delicate balance. Stanley had obviously been having a bad time and could look forward to no appreciable improvement in the immediate future.

"We were sitting on our back steps," Stanley said, "and we saw the light go on next door. What's doing up there?"

"It's the police," Jack said dreamily. "Masters, I suppose. He must be looking for something."

"Looking for what?"

"I don't know. Nancy thinks it's a key to the back door. Maybe it's for some evidence that you were in the room the night Lila was killed. Did you leave any fingerprints, Stanley?"

"My God, Jack, don't say things like that! You know I was only at the door. I wasn't inside at all."

"I know? How? Because you say so?"

"It's the truth. I swear! I was called down to police headquarters and I told the lieutenant exactly what happened."

"You were a long time telling it, pal. Masters is pretty hard to bamboozle."

Stanley was temporarily speechless.

"Anything that happens to him will serve him right," Mae Walters said contemptuously. "He knew I'd taken a sleeping pill—that's why he felt free to prowl around half the night talking to women in nightgowns—if she *wore* a nightgown."

"We have been over that and over it," Stanley spluttered, "and I don't want to go over it again—"

"It's probable that you will go over it again whether you want to or not," Mae said. "Murdering Lila isn't the only thing you could have done to her. For instance, you have shown that you'll lie your fat head off at the drop of a bra."

"Well," Stanley said bitterly, "you just be sure to tell Masters that. He'll be interested in the opinion of my own *wife*."

"Oh, cut it out, Mae," Jack said. "I was only pulling Stanley's leg. Or maybe engaging in a little wishful thinking. Whatever he's looking for, I'm the one Masters is gunning for."

"What makes you think so?" Nancy asked suddenly.

"I don't think, Nancy, I know. When the murder-suicide theory began to pop holes, I knew it was only a matter of time until he got around to me. He's already been asking questions about me at the hospital. Other places, too, no doubt."

"Let him ask," David said heartily. "You were at the hospital that night, Jack, and you can prove it."

"I can't prove I didn't leave for a while. And that's not all of it. There's something else he'll find out, if he hasn't already. You ought to be satisfied with old Stanley, Mae. You might have been married to me."

"You're married to me, as I recall," Vera said, "and if I've had any complaints you're the only one I've expressed them to."

"That's true, dear, and I'm grateful. Well, what will be will be. Any case Masters works out against me has to be highly circumstantial. The most he can show is that I *could* have committed murder, not that I did. I ought to be able to beat the rap with a good lawyer."

"It would ruin your life," Vera said. "Who'd go to a doctor acquitted of murder?"

"More than would go to one convicted of it. Anyway, there's always research or veterinary medicine."

At that moment the light went out next door. The three couples sat in the deepening dusk in silence, waiting; and after a few minutes, sure enough, the back door of the Connor house opened and Lieutenant Masters appeared. It was quite dark by now, and Masters was blurry in the shadows; he seemed to be doing something to the back door, which he had pulled shut behind him. His mysterious activity soon became clear: the door opened again. He had unlocked it from the outside.

"He's found it," Nancy exclaimed. "He's found the lost key!"

As he turned from the door, Masters noticed them watching him from the Richmond terrace. He came immediately toward them. It was apparent that he had been engaged in some strenuous labor. His tie was hanging limply from his open collar, on his face was a smear of dirt where it had been caked by perspiration. He was holding the key in his right hand. He began to toss and catch it deliberately.

"Good evening," he said in a peculiar tone.

"Somehow," said Nancy, "I have a notion that it isn't."

"I wouldn't want to spoil your get-together, Mrs. Howell. I can see you all later if you prefer. Or rather the one I want particularly to see."

"No, thank you, I, for one, would rather not have to wait and wonder. Can't you advance the time of execution?"

"I agree," Jack Richmond said. "Even the guilty sleep better if things are settled."

"In that case," Masters said, "since you're the one I want particularly to see, Doctor, I'll be glad to oblige."

"That sounds ominous. Am I going to be arrested for something?"

"Are you confessing to something?"

"Not at all. Would you sit down, Lieutenant?"

"Thank you."

"How civilized we're all being," sneered Mae Walters.

"Shut up," said Stanley Walters savagely. His tone so startled his wife that she shut up.

David Howell said, "My wife guessed that you were looking for Larry's back-door key, Lieutenant. I see you've found it."

"That's right, Mr. Howell."

"I don't know *how*," Nancy said. "The other morning you and I looked and looked for it, Lieutenant, and we didn't find it."

"That was because we didn't look in the right place."

"Where was the right place, if it isn't classified information?"

"Exactly where I suspected," said Masters, not without satisfaction. "Remember, just as we were leaving, I mentioned having a notion? I got it at the last moment, while I was in the upstairs bathroom. When I opened the medicine cabinet above the washbowl, I noticed the little slot in the cabinet for the disposal of used razor blades. It occurred to me that the razor slot would be a great place for someone to dispose of a key he didn't want found, and this evening I came back to dig that razor receptacle out. I was right. I found the key lying among a flock of old blades."

"That was clever of you, Lieutenant," said Vera Richmond, "jumping to the conclusion that the key had been dropped in there."

"It wasn't entirely a guess, Mrs. Richmond. The slot is very narrow, and a more careful examination indicated that something had been forced through it recently."

"Good work, Lieutenant," Jack Richmond said. "As my wife says, you've been clever."

"I'm afraid I can't say as much for our murderer," said Masters genially. "He made several bad mistakes, and hiding this key was one of them. If he'd just left it lying around, I'd have no special reason to attach any significance to it. By trying to dispose of it, he only called attention to it. Now we know as a fact that he used it to gain entry to the house."

"And then left the door unlocked when he made his getaway?" Dr. Jack Richmond said.

"He had to do that. He wanted Lila Connor's body found as quickly as was compatible with his deception regarding the times of death. He counted on someone's becoming uneasy and insisting on entering the house, and an unlocked back door greased the way. Incidentally, if Mrs. Howell hadn't insisted on investigating, my guess is the murderer would have done so."

"That's the same as saying that the murderer is in this neighborhood, Lieutenant."

"Closer than that, Doctor. He's on this terrace."

There was a dampish silence. Finally Jack Richmond said, "Well, so now what?"

"I'm in no hurry, Doctor," said Masters comfortably;

Nancy *hated* him. "Would you folks like to know how these murders were pulled off?"

"I'd like to know how you *think* they were pulled off," snapped Nancy. "That might not come to the same thing."

"I'll be happy to listen to any contrary opinion after I've finished, Mrs. Howell," said the detective with a little nod. "Well, to begin with, let's assume—just to give us a handle to this thing—let's assume the murderer was you, Dr. Richmond."

"Me," said Jack. "All right, let's."

"You spotted Larry Connor leaving his house on what proved to be the night of the crimes. You must have heard him talking to Mrs. Howell outside, because events show that you knew exactly where he was going— and you did say, didn't you, that the windows of your house here were open that night? Probably you had not yet committed yourself to a program of murder and hocus-pocus. That decision must have come later, when you got a call to come to the hospital and found, after getting there, that you were in for a long wait. The wait presented you with the opportunity, and the rest was brainwork."

"I sound like a veritable monster," said Jack.

Masters smiled. "It was a simple matter to arrange for an empty private room to 'rest' in. The relative location of the room made it equally simple to slip out and down the stairway and go back unseen later. There was a considerable element of risk, of course. But you'd be safe if you could get back to the room before you were called to your patient—whom you'd examined and whose condition told you roughly how much time you had. You must have estimated that you had over an hour. So you sneaked out and drove to Larry Connor's office.

"He had had a bad time, and you were a doctor and his 'friend.' You persuaded him to take a sedative and you prepared it yourself. But it was no sedative. You gave him a highly undoctorish Mickey Finn, in a lethal dose, to confuse the trail back to you. You then set the office scene to indicate suicide, did three further things, and hurried back to the hospital before you could be missed.

"The three things you had to do constituted the heart of your plan. Lila Connor, not her husband, was your primary target. Therefore you had to make it appear that Larry died *after* Lila died—in spite of the fact that at this point Lila was still alive. You accomplished the first part of this deception by turning Larry's office air-conditioning up as high as it would go, to slow the rate of decomposition; this meant, of course, that you had to return to the office early Sunday morning, before Larry's body could be discovered, to turn the air-conditioner *off*, thereby establishing the presumption that it had never been on at all; otherwise, allowance would have been made for the air-conditioning factor and negated your deception. Secondly, the weapon which was to kill Lila had to bear his fingerprints. This was simple: you took the metal letter-opener from his desk, pressed the fingers of his right hand to the haft, carefully wrapped the letter-opener so as not to erase the prints, and carried it off with you in your medical bag. Thirdly, you took Connor's back-door house key from his keycase, so that you could be sure of access to the Connor ·house—and Lila Connor—after you got through with your patient at the hospital and could drive home."

"That's a beautiful reconstruction, Lieutenant," said Dr. Richmond. "Do you do your homework with detective stories? Fortunately, real life requires evidence."

"You let me worry about that, will you, Doctor?" said Masters with a smile. "Even at that, it's not all theorizing. I can prove that the air-conditioner in Larry Connor's office was turned on and, much later, off. The night watchman heard the conditioner working when he made his second rounds of the night, and he'll swear to it. I myself can testify, with the landlord of the building to bear me out, since he was with me, that the air-conditioner was off when we discovered Connor's body. Meaning that the murderer had to have come back to the office, as I 'theorized.'

"As for the weapon, Connor was strictly left-handed. On that score alone he's cleared of the murder of his wife. It was a bad mistake to forget that fact in salting the letter-opener with the prints of Connor's right hand —even allowing for the natural tensions of the night, the need to hurry, and so on. Yet the letter-opener came from Connor's office desk—his secretary will positively identify it as such. Obviously, somebody other than Connor took the letter-knife from the office to the Connor house, and since we found it buried in Lila Connor's breast, it was just as obviously taken by the murderer from the office for that purpose."

Jack Richmond was thoughtfully examining his empty beer can. Then he looked up. "Actually, Lieutenant, you make out a beautiful case, but not against me necessarily. You haven't demonstrated a single piece of direct evidence to link *me* to either death. It's all circumstantial."

"A lot of people have found themselves at the end of a rope, or in some equally unpleasant place," said Masters dryly, "as a result of circumstantial evidence. Also, there's the little matter of motive."

Jack Richmond stirred, and Masters fell silent. He was silent for so long that he seemed to them to have been sidetracked by some faint far thought that switched on unexpectedly in the twilight.

"Do you want me to go into your motive, Dr. Richmond?" he said at last.

"You *have* been busy, Lieutenant, haven't you?" murmured Jack. He laughed harshly. "All right, I was fool enough to let myself get involved with Lila. It was all over quite a while before she died. Don't expect me to go into the details. You probably know most of them, anyhow."

"I've made some run-producing hits," nodded Masters. "See here, Doctor, if you'd rather not discuss this before your wife—"

"Don't let Mrs. Richmond's presence embarrass you, Lieutenant. My wife has known all about Lila and me for a long time. I'm happy to say that Vera knows because I told her, not because she caught me. So why should I have killed Lila? What price motive now?"

Masters blinked. He turned to Vera Richmond. "Is that the truth, Mrs. Richmond? And please don't say it is if your husband is lying. It wouldn't do either him or you any good, and if repeated officially it could have nasty consequences for you."

"Jack told me voluntarily," Vera said steadily. "And I decided not to let it break us up. For two reasons, Lieutenant. One, I love him. Two, I know he loves me, in spite of an occasional lapse of fidelity. It seemed to me ridiculous to allow our marriage to be ruined because of a tramp who didn't mean anything to him but a fling."

"That makes you out a rather remarkable woman, Mrs. Richmond. Wasn't it pretty rough on you, having to live next door to the woman your husband confessed he'd been sleeping with?"

Vera flushed. But her voice did not quiver. "Yes, Lieutenant, it was rough, especially since for the sake of appearances we had to maintain a social relationship with the Connors. But what would you have had me do? Run? Tell Jack we had to move? It would only have given Lila a satisfaction she didn't deserve. And after all, any way you look at it, I won and she lost."

"Very refreshing attitude," snapped Masters. "But it sounds a little too superhuman to suit me. I still think your husband's affair with Lila Connor gave him a motive to kill her."

"But how?" asked Vera, and this time it was a cry of protest. "He was through with her—I knew about it—"

"Was any man ever finished with Lila Connor," said Masters in a deliberately brutal tone, "until *she* was ready to let go?"

His tone, his phrasing, seemed to bring Lila back, as by obscene invocation, from the dead. In the shadows Jack Richmond sighed.

"Apparently," he said, "you investigated Lila thoroughly."

"Yes, Doctor. The night of your party Larry Connor was reported to have made some harsh and startling comments about his wife. You surely didn't expect me to ignore them? I checked on them, and they were all true. Lila had had three husbands in rapid succession before her marriage to Connor, and she played hell with all three. As she continued to do in the Connor marriage. She seems to have been driven by a hatred of men. She apparently got her kicks by entangling men emotionally, then dropping them with a thud. The only thing she couldn't take was *being* dropped. Then she became really dangerous. Exactly what kind of threat did she pose when you went sour on her, Doctor? Scandal? Professional ruin? What did she want from you? Money? Divorce and remarriage?"

"I didn't have enough money to satisfy her, and I would rather have married an octopus."

"You admit, then, that she threatened you!"

"I don't admit a thing. As for my reputation and professional career, important as they are to me, I wouldn't kill because of a threat to them, expressed or implied."

"Wouldn't you? *Didn't* you?"

"I wouldn't, and I didn't. You haven't got a case, Lieutenant, admit it. It's all based on what I could have done, not on what I did. As for that two hours or so at the hospital, I repeat that I was in that private room napping every second of the unaccounted-for time, and I challenge you to prove otherwise."

"I'll prove it if I can, and I think I can."

"Are you saying that I'm under arrest?"

"Arrest?" Masters seemed to consider the question. "No. Not yet, Dr. Richmond."

"That's what I thought." Jack laughed and rose abruptly. "You'll have to excuse me. This has been something of a strain."

Without another word he turned and went into his house. Vera followed him quickly, looking worried. Masters continued to sit there for a few moments, then he slapped his thigh and said, "I'm sorry. By God, I'm sorry," but whether this was a reference to the Richmonds or to his own position was not clear. He jumped up and left. These abrupt departures left the Walterses and the Howells rather awkwardly abandoned on the Richmond terrace.

"I knew it," Mae said. "I knew from the start that Lila was a tramp."

"Shut up, Mae," Stanley said.

"She was bound to come to a bad end."

"*Shut up, Mae,*" Stanley said.

"Yes, Mae," Nancy said. "Do, please!"

"Come on, Stanley," Mae said. "It's apparent that we had better go home."

Stanley rose without haste and walked Mae across the yard to the alley. On the way, Mae took his arm.

"Stanley Rides Again," Nancy murmured. "He's practically pure by comparison."

"Mae's impossible. I'd rather not talk about her."

"Not Vera, though. Vera is superb. I wonder what I'd do if I caught you playing around."

"You'd do just what I did about you and Stanley in the alley," said David. "You'd adjust."

"I was just joking about that, David Howell, and you know it!"

"In that case, let's drop it. I feel like hell, tootsypuss, and all I want is to go home and hoist a few."

So the Howells went home and hoisted a few, and so forth, finally wrapping themselves around each other in an obscure revulsion from the death, dissolution and adultery of the evening's conversation.

15

Masters was not happy. He had slept poorly for three nights; his temper was short, his tolerance level low. He was even, in a rational sort of way, hearing voices when he was alone, or rather, a voice. He heard it over and over, the voice of Jack Richmond. He was hearing it now, as he sat brooding at his desk.

"I was in that private room napping every second of the unaccounted-for time," the voice of Jack Richmond said, *"and I challenge you to prove otherwise."*

Each time he heard the unvoiced words, they sounded more like the bluster of a guilty man. They did not sound at all, in Masters's judgment, like the despair of innocence. They seemed the vain utterance of a man who was getting away with something. Masters did indeed feel challenged.

The hell of it was—the blazing, frustrating hell of it was—that the doctor was perfectly right in one respect. He had gone into an empty hospital room before Larry Connor's murder, and he had been found there over an hour later, and there was no way of proving that he had not remained there the whole time. For three days Masters had tried in vain to dig up a witness who had seen Dr. Richmond during the crucial period. He had apparently not been seen approaching the Connor office, or leaving it, or returning and leaving Sunday morning for the legerdemain with the air-conditioner. It was bad luck. The streets of the town early on a Sunday morning would have been virtually deserted. As, apparently, they had been.

Masters was still at his desk, brooding, when his chief dropped in and claimed a chair.

"How's it going, Gus?"

"It's not," Masters said. "It's gone. Gone, I mean, as far as it's going."

"You decided to drop it? You think, after all, it was murder and suicide by Connor?"

The chief's voice betrayed the wish behind the thought, and Masters's recognition of it increased his irritation.

"Hell, no. It wasn't murder and suicide by Connor, and I haven't decided to drop it. Damn it all, you can't just drop a murder case."

"Don't get upset, Gus," said the chief, with the sympathy of a man who has slid home safely and can afford to relax. "Any plans?"

"To slit my throat, maybe. I know what happened, and I know who's guilty. And I can't do a damn thing about it!"

"Who's *guilty*?" repeated the chief, astounded. "Who, who?"

"Dr. Jack Richmond, that's who. I'll give odds on it." Masters added, "Though there don't seem to be any takers."

"If you know he's guilty—"

"There's a big difference between knowing something and proving it. There's no proof."

"You'd better be sure," said the chief excitedly. "We can't afford a mistake that big."

Masters grunted.

"I've got a suggestion, Gus. You listening?"

"I'm listening."

"Dump what you've got on the county attorney's desk. Let *him* decide if it's anything he wants to take into court."

"The county attorney," Masters said wearily, "is just a few years out of law school, and his trial experience doesn't include first-degree murder. You expect that pup to take a chance on getting his brains knocked out? He wouldn't even try."

"Damn it, Gus, you fish or cut bait. You can't spend the rest of your life on this thing!"

"Look, Chief, let me keep up the pressure on this guy. He may break. or something. If I could only dream up a way to trick him into exposing himself!"

"On your head be it," said the chief oracularly. He heaved himself to his feet, creaking in various places. "Because you can lose it, Masters, if you do anything foolish."

He left; and Masters, abandoned in his own unpleasant company, reflected on the ominous change in his chief's form of address from "Gus" to "Masters." There was nothing very subtle about the warning that accompanied it. But then the chief had not retained his office for sixteen years by the exercise of subtlety. Wham! was his motto.

So now, the lieutenant thought, my job is on the line, too.

But Augustus Masters was a stubborn man. As he saw it, he had no choices. Back to the wars.

He decided to try to cleanse his mind of all bias and preconception and go over the case from as virgin a viewpoint as he could muster. Forget Dr. Jack Richmond and all the fancy deductions about the air-conditioning. forget everything but the facts, and even reexamine those for hidden flaws or rivulets that trickled off in unguessed directions.

The logical place to start, he thought, was Larry Connor's office. He had kept it locked; it was as the investigation had left it. Doggedly Masters reached for his hat and walked over to the business block and entered the alley running behind it.

He let himself in by way of the alley door and stood for a moment in the hot storeroom behind Connor's office. The air was stale and stifling, and he automatically jerked his collar open and loosened his tie. The air-conditioner in the window beside him was silent, and he found himself listening in the silence. He was aware of a vague and irrational uneasiness. This was ridiculous, of course, and he started to laugh; but then he was listening hard, crouched a little. There *was* a sound, an odd sound scarcely more audible than heavy breathing; and after a moment he realized that someone, somewhere on the premises, was crying.

Masters moved his bulk with remarkable swiftness. He was across the storeroom and in the central office in a flash. But no one was there. The outer office, then . . . He had almost reached it when the muffled crying stopped, as if from sheer exhaustion. He yanked the door open; and there, in the drape-drawn, dusty anteroom, at her useless desk, sat Ruth Benton, arms on the desk and head on her arms. She raised her head on hearing him; her face was swollen and red and a muddle of ruined make-up. She seemed not in the least startled —as if, somehow, she had been expecting him. It was Masters who was startled; he had forgotten that she had a key to Connor's office.

"Miss Benton," he said softly. "What are you doing here?"

Larry Connor's secretary either did not know or did not care what her face revealed. "I came to get some of my things," she said in a dreary way. "I didn't think I'd mind. But when I got here and saw the dust, the . . . decay, and realized . . ." Ruth Benton shrugged. "It got me. I broke down and cried like a baby. Just like a woman. Eh, Lieutenant?"

"Sometimes I wish I could break down and cry like a baby myself," said Masters. "It's nothing to be ashamed of."

"Oh, I'm over it now," the girl said. "I suppose I'm trespassing. I'm sorry if I've broken a rule or something. I won't come back again."

"Just leave your key, Miss Benton."

"I've already put it in the drawer here. Do you want to check what I'm taking? They're all personal possessions."

"That won't be necessary," said Masters, nevertheless looking over the litter of compacts, hairpins, tissues, ball-point pens and such things that the girl had spread on the desk. She began putting them into her purse. "You must have thought a lot of Larry Connor."

"More than he thought of me, I'm afraid," she said.

"How do you figure that, Miss Benton?"

"He killed himself, didn't he?"

"Do you have much trouble accepting the idea that he killed his wife?"

"I don't want to talk about *that.*"

"Please," said Masters, and she looked up at him, faintly frowning. "Suppose I told you that he didn't?"

"Didn't what?"

"Kill his wife."

"Oh." Her shoulders drooped again. "You mean because of the letter-opener? He could have taken it home the day before or something. I couldn't swear that he didn't."

"How long had it been on his desk?"

"Years. It was here when I came to work for him."

"And suddenly he took it home? Anyway, we have reason to believe someone was with him in this office the night Larry Connor died."

"Why are you telling me this? Do you think it was me?"

"Was it?"

"No," Ruth Benton said. "I wish it had been. He might still be alive."

"Do you have any notion of who it was?"

"Not the slightest."

Masters looked around. "Have you been in the inner office since you came?"

"No. I don't believe I could bear going in there."

Masters let her out and relocked the street door. He put out the anteroom light and went into Larry Connor's office.

He looked for a moment at the sofa. Then he trudged into the lavatory, where he went through the medicine cabinet again. It yielded nothing; he returned to the office.

He sat down behind Larry Connor's desk and dug in.

Nothing came to him, absolutely nothing. He thought and thought, and his thoughts ranged over territory that was merely familiar and barren. He began to curse the choking heat.

And suddenly he was aware that he had been staring at the telephone on Larry Connor's desk. The telephone. *The telephone!*

He had completely ignored the telephone.

He began to think in terms of telephone. It led him back over a sinuous course. After he had thought the whole thing through, he put his thoughts together in orderly fashion.

Larry Connor‚had left home that night, after a quarrel with his wife, at midnight or a little after—Nancy Howell had not recalled the exact time. No matter; more important was the time Larry had arrived at his office.

If he had driven there directly from his home, not more than ten minutes or so should have elapsed. But suppose he had not come directly? A man with Connor's troubles and in Connor's frame of mind might well have made for a bar. Masters had dropped the stop-in-at-a-bar theory because no bartender in any of the fringe joints that violated the closing-hour ordinance had testified to having seen him. Understandable.

So understandable, in fact, that their testimony was

worthless. Of course the barkeepers would have denied seeing the man who was now dead and the center of a small-town sensation! Why get involved and upset the fine balance by which such outside-the-law joints remained in business?

Assume, then, that Larry Connor *had* stopped in at some joint to get loaded. And some of them, particularly the ones in which the pimps and prostitutes hung out, were pretty low; a drunk could get himself into a peck of trouble. Knockout drops were far from unknown. A big bill could buy some—if not from the bar, then from some unsavory character sitting at it. If a man were desperate enough . . .

It led, astonishingly, back to the idea that maybe Larry Connor had committed suicide after all. (Forget the Lila kill, Masters told himself sternly; for now forget it. And the air-conditioning. *Stick to Connor in that office.*)

Say that Larry Connor decided to take his own life, and bought some chloral hydrate for that purpose, simply because he had reached the point where death was preferable to going on living. He had come back here to this hot room, clutching the chloral hydrate, and he had mixed his lethal Mickey Finn, and he had swallowed it and lain down on the sofa there to wait for unconsciousness and death.

Now: Larry versus Lila and the Lila kill. He had not killed her. That was certain, from the wrong-hand prints on the murder weapon. Somebody else had used that weapon, putting Larry's prints on it . . . *somebody who could not have done so unless Larry was already dead.* That placed Lila's killer in this office, with Larry dead or lapsing into death—someone who had come here after Larry voluntarily swallowed the overdose of chloral hydrate. The killer had to have been here in order to get possession of Connor's letter-knife, in order to press

Connor's prints on it and tag him for a murder he never dreamed of committing.

Larry had been a dead patsy.

But if the murderer of Lila had not been responsible also for Larry's death, at least in the sense of having planned it, how the devil had he known that Larry was dying, or dead, in the office? And with Larry dying or dead, how had the unknown gained entrance to the office? True, there was that key to the street door, *not* Larry Connor's own . . . the key just deposited in the outer-office desk drawer by . . .

Ruth Benton.

Masters considered Ruth Benton.

Larry's secretary had been in love with her boss. What would she have done if she had discovered his body in the office that night, obviously self-destroyed, driven to suicide by his vicious wife? Would Ruth, in grief and rage, have gone hunting for Lila Connor's scalp? In her overwrought state, would she have been capable of the elaborate deceptions Lila's killer engaged in? And aside from all that . . . a "chance" visit to the office after midnight Saturday night was uncomfortably coincidental, although coincidence could never be ruled out. Still, Masters recoiled from it. There was too much in this tricky case that showed design. No, he could not buy accidental discovery of the suicide. But suppose . . . suppose the visit had *not* been by accident. Suppose . . . *suppose Larry Connor had called her.*

The telephone.

The telephone might be the key to all the mysteries!

A man takes a drug that will kill him—takes it deliberately—and lies down to die. How many would-be suicides, sure that they want death, experience an abrupt change of heart at the approach of the grim reality? It was an everyday occurrence—police files and hospital records were full of such cases.

Suppose, after swallowing the drug and feeling its first effects, Larry Connor had become frantically certain that he did not want to die after all?

Suppose he had telephoned for help?

Masters sat hunched over Larry Connor's desk, exulting. He had the feeling. It was like swimming after a long layoff, lungs heaving, arms like lead weights, and then, without warning . . . second wind, breaths easy, no weight, streaking for the nearing shore like a fish. He had the feeling.

The drug has been taken. Larry Connor lies on the sofa waiting to die. As he waits, death becomes dreadful. He begins to feel terror. In spite of everything, he wants to live. And to live he needs help, desperately, quickly, for the drug is already taking effect.

He is groggy now, his thoughts tumbling, his mind clogged. Here is the telephone at hand . . . can he make it? He struggles off the sofa, manages to get to the desk, unhook the phone. He will call . . . whom? Perhaps he knows; perhaps he tries. But he cannot remember the number, or he is not coordinating—his forefinger like a swollen thumb on the dial. What would he do?

Call Operator. Surely he could manage one swing of the dial.

Operator answers. He asks *her* to dial . . . whom? Ruth Benton? Dying, needing help, would he have summoned Ruth Benton?

No. A man dying of an overdose of a drug he has himself taken would grasp at only one savior.

A doctor.

His doctor?

Masters sat back. He did not have to answer the question. It could be answered by the operator at the telephone exchange. She would remember the call, to whom it had been placed.

She would. Masters was sure she would. He no more questioned his certainty than he questioned the whole train of thought that had led him to it.

This was right. This was it.

16

He pressed the button and listened to the harmony of the chimes. The sun blazed in a sky of brilliant blue. The chimes died, and after a moment he aimed his index finger and jabbed again, again listening and glancing at the sun. Still no one came. He had better try the back door.

No one responded to his knock at the back door, either.

He looked off to his right, across the intervening Connor backyard, to the backyard of the Howells. The chances were good that Nancy Howell was at home, and he thought that he would go and bother her just once more.

He could see, when Nancy came to her door, that he was not welcome. He felt regret and loneliness, but he shut them out. He was far too old and jaded to regret what could not be helped, or to try to recover what had long been lost.

"Good morning," Masters said. "I'm sorry to have to disturb you again."

"I should hope you would be," Nancy said. "I should hope you'd be ashamed to disturb me again, ever. I've tried my best to help you, and it's only brought grief to people I like and respect."

"I'm the one who has brought the grief, Mrs. Howell, not you. It's inseparable from the job."

"It's a rotten job, that's all I can say!"

"A very rotten job. But somebody has to do it. The other night at the Richmonds', for example. Do you think I enjoyed that?"

"You were the worst kind of bully, Lieutenant Masters."

"Bully!" This manifest injustice caused Master's voice to skid slightly. "Oh, well. Perhaps I was. I don't blame you for thinking so. But I'll cut this short. Do you happen to know where the Richmonds are? They don't answer either front or back."

"Well, Jack is a doctor," Nancy said coldly, "and it's reasonable to assume that he's out doctoring."

"How about Mrs. Richmond?"

"If Vera isn't home, I don't know where she is. Maybe she went downtown or to the market."

"Well, I think I'll try to track down Dr. Richmond."

"I wish I could wish you luck, but I don't."

"Thanks," Masters said sadly, "for wishing you could wish."

He had been holding his hat in his hand. Now he set it squarely on his balding head and made off around the Howell house to the street and across the street to his car. He could hear the spiteful slam of the Howells' back door. She didn't even ask me in, he thought. He got into his car and drove downtown.

Dr. Jack Richmond's office was located in the new Medical Arts Building, a mathematical one-story structure of glass and green brick set behind a lawn so lush it looked artificial. Masters shuffled through the lobby past the gleaming pharmacy and along a long sterile-looking corridor to the all-wood door with "John R. Richmond, M.D." richly spelled out in stainless steel letters. Masters went in.

The waiting room was empty.

"Dr. Richmond is not in," the sharp-chinned receptionist in the glassed-in cubicle said. "Do you have an appointment?"

"This isn't a medical call," Masters said. He opened his badge case, and her eyes narrowed. "Where is he?"

"He's usually back from the hospital at this hour," the receptionist said, "but he called in to say he had an emergency and didn't know when he'd be back."

"An emergency at the hospital?"

"I really couldn't say."

"Look, sister," Masters said patiently. "Every doctor's assistant knows where he is every minute. Is he at the hospital?"

"I think so." She was frightened. "Yes."

Masters drove over to the hospital. Dr. Richmond was in surgery. An emergency appendectomy. He would have to wait.

Masters cursed under his breath. He loitered. He read the posted hospital rules. He studied a large print showing a group of frock-coated men stooping over a cadaverous-looking naked man on a rough kitchen table, a picture labeled *The Surgeons*. He leafed through some magazines.

Suddenly he could stand the waiting no longer. He hurried to the elevators. One car was open, and he strode in and punched the number five button. The elevator door closed at a snail's pace. The ascent to the top floor was interminable.

Lieutenant Masters took up his vigil outside the big double door of the operating theater.

His back to the wall.

Symbolically.

17

First there was Lila, Nancy thought, now Vera.

Were people to be forever disappearing from Shady Acres? It gave a person the creepiest feeling.

Of course, it was nonsense to think of Vera as having "disappeared." She had merely gone out. Right now she was probably downtown shopping at Logan's, or at the supermarket; or maybe she was at the beauty parlor. There were scads of places she could have gone for perfectly good reasons; certainly there was no cause to feel uneasy about her. It was that damned Lieutenant Masters's fault. Every time he turned up he brought a whiff of doom with him. Vera was fine.

Nevertheless, in the first hour following Masters's departure, Nancy found a dozen excuses for glancing over to the Richmond house. There was no sign of Vera. But one would hardly expect her to run up a flag to show she was back home. She might have returned at any time during the hour. If so, she had probably left her Volkswagen, the little second car she drove when Jack was off in the Corvette, parked in her drive.

Nancy went to the living room and looked out.

The Volkswagen was not in the Richmond drive or at the curb.

Vera could have run it into the garage, of course. Well, there was nothing to be gained from speculating about it, Nancy told herself. The sensible thing to do was to phone Vera on some pretext or other, just to make sure she was all right.

Nancy went to the phone in the hall and dialed the Richmond number.

She waited through eight rings. There was no answer. Nancy hung up.

Vera simply wasn't at home. But then why did Nancy persist in having the nagging feeling that she *was?*

It could be that Vera, for her own reasons, just wasn't answering the door or the phone. No, that wasn't likely. Vera was a well-trained doctor's wife; any call might be important . . .

Nancy's feeling of uneasiness began to assume the shape of alarm. Call it unreasonable, call it absurd, call it anything, it had grown too disturbing to be tolerated. She would either have to put it out of her mind, which was impossible, or do something about it.

The first thing Nancy did was to run across the street to the Richmonds' attached garage. The overhead door was closed, but there were three tiny windows that Nancy could just look through by standing on tiptoe. She stretched and looked, and there in the garage stood the Volkswagen. If Vera had gone somewhere, she had either walked or been driven there by Jack. But Vera hated walking, and Jack usually left for the hospital or his office long before Vera got out of bed . . .

Nancy went around to the back door. She hesitated only a moment. Then she turned the knob and, timidly, pushed. To her surprise the door swung inward. Unlocked, with Vera away?

Nancy stepped into Vera Richmond's kitchen. The conditioned air was cool and delightfully dry, and it made her feel light and liberated. At the same time she was oppressed by a dragging dread that made every step an act of will.

She held her breath and, cocking her head, paused

to listen. But there was nothing to hear. It sounded exactly like an empty house, soundless.

Nevertheless, Nancy called, "Ver-aaa?" and waited. "Vera! You home?"

There was no answer. Nancy forced herself to go into the entrance hall.

"Vera?"

No answer.

I wonder, Nancy thought, what I would say if the front door opened this minute and Vera walked in. How do you explain being caught in your neighbor's house? She laughed with vexation. The hell with that. There was something wrong, and she knew it. Nancy went determinedly into the Richmonds' sunken living room.

It was a beautiful room, which Nancy had secretly envied for a long time. But she felt no envy now. Her attention fixed on the massive bleached mahogany door at the other end. For some reason. For some reason.

Behind that door was Jack Richmond's study.

Behind that door lay something dreadful. Nancy knew it. She did not know how she knew it, but she knew it.

Like a sleepwalker she moved across the living room and opened the heavy door and looked into Jack Richmond's study and there was Vera Richmond as Nancy had known in her heart she would be. Vera Richmond was in a big high-backed leather chair facing the door, almost as if she were expecting someone to come in and was sitting there quietly, waiting. But she was dead.

She was dead, and Nancy was so sure she was dead that she did not advance one quarter-step into the study. She just stood there and looked at her friend with an odd sense of detachment, all urgency ended.

Vera had brushed her hair and touched up her lips and cheeks and got into a crisp bright summer frock in preparation for her death. She looked quite pretty, Nancy thought. And utterly serene. The drapes were drawn back from the picture window behind her, and the sunshine through the Venetian slats fashioned a stairway of light across the glowing parquet floor . . . a stairway from life to death. It was really a lovely room to die in.

Vera was dead.

Vera dead? It was unthinkable. Vera had always been there, quiet, smiling, efficient, self-effacing; "my third arm," as Jack used to say. Vera was the kind of person who just went on forever.

But here she was, suddenly, impossibly, inexplicably dead in her husband's chair. And the question, after all, was why. Surely she hadn't brushed her hair and got into a freshly ironed dress and made her face up just to sit down and die on a beautiful summer morning. Surely she hadn't! But she had. She had died for a reason of her own, in her own way and time.

Turning violently, Nancy saw the desk of rubbed mahogany, its matching chair pushed back as if someone had just risen from it and walked away. And someone had. Vera. For on the desk, under a blue glass weight, lay two sheets of white paper filled with Vera's bold script. She had sat down there to write something before dying, perhaps while waiting to die; and there it was, under the weight . . .

With some surprise Nancy found herself at the desk. She was not aware of having crossed the study; suddenly she was there. And pushing the glass weight aside with the tips of her fingernails, and stooping over the desk without touching the papers, and reading what Vera had written.

Jack darling:
    Ever since the other night on our terrace, I have known with the most terrible certainty that Lieutenant Masters would come back. This morning he came. He rang the front door bell, and then he

went around to the back. But I did not answer and after a while he went away. So I know what I must do. Forgive me, darling, as I forgave you.

I know it is only a matter of time, and I am tired of waiting. What I should have realized from the beginning was that you would be blamed and that in the end, found out or not, I would have to save you. You knew all along, of course, what I had done. But you never accused me, you never condemned me, and I'm so grateful for that. You will not forget, I hope, that I tried indirectly to assure you that I would never let you suffer for my mistake.

It *was* a mistake. I realized that as soon as it was made, but by then it was too late. Masters is shrewd. He had everything almost right except the all-important fact that it was I, not you, who was guilty. Larry phoned that night from his office. He wanted you. He had taken the overdose, as I'll be doing soon, but he had become frightened, changed his mind, and wanted help. You were out on that emergency, I knew every second counted, I'd been a nurse, so I went to him myself.

I'm sorry about Larry. I sincerely meant to help him if I could. But when I reached his office, getting in through the back door that somehow he'd managed to unlock for me, I found him deep in coma on the sofa. That was when, in one blinding flash of revelation, I saw how I could rid you and me of Lila once for all without—I thought—being involved. With Larry having swallowed poison, he would be blamed for killing her . . . Anyway, I stood there in that office and watched and waited as Larry died. I don't know if I could have saved him in any event; he was very far gone when I got there. But maybe that's just rationalizing. The point is, I let him die without trying to save his life. By doing *nothing* I murdered him as surely, I suppose—I suppose—as if I had forced him to swallow the drug in the first place.

Lila I killed with my own hand. When I got back home there was still a light in her bedroom, and I had to wait for her to go to sleep. It was very risky, because I didn't know exactly when you might return from the hospital; and the truth is, I had no more than finished and got into bed when you got home. I'm not sorry about having killed Lila, I'm only sorry that everything has come out badly for you and me. Lila's greatest mistake was not understanding what *I* was. She was beginning to threaten me in a dozen different ways, to taunt me. Did she honestly think that I would take it? After all she'd done to me through you?

There would be no point in repeating the details of how I killed her, the air-conditioning business, and all the rest of it. Masters has already worked it out, and he has been wrong in nothing except, as I said, the identity of the one responsible. And I'm pretty sure, after his visit this morning, that he is no longer wrong in even that.

Jack darling, you said that you were neither a coward nor a fool, but I have been both . . .

That was not the end of the letter, but Nancy stopped reading. She turned away with a whimper that froze in her throat.

Jack Richmond was standing in the doorway. He was not looking at Nancy; he seemed hardly aware that she was there. He was looking at his wife in the chair with the lusterless eyes of an old man. His face was gray, and his voice, when he finally spoke, was without inflection or, indeed, any human character.

"She's dead," he said.

It was not a statement that called for a reply, and

Nancy was wordless. Then she looked up, and there, behind Jack Richmond, stood Lieutenant Masters. He had been there all the time.

But it was not the presence of Masters that made Nancy come to life and run blindly from the room. It was something Jack Richmond said.

Vera's husband looked up at Nancy, and he said in the most chillingly courteous way, "I'm sure you will excuse us now?"

Afterward, when Masters came out of the study, he went over to where he had asked Nancy to sit and wait in the living room, and he said to her, "I'm sorry I asked you to wait, Mrs. Howell. You look like death yourself. I can take your statement later. Can you get home all right?" He was a little stooped in her direction, in an attitude of deference, or supplication, as if mutely pleading his innocence.

But Nancy said, "Is it true?"

"Is what true, Mrs. Howell?"

"That when you came here this morning you were really coming for Vera?"

"Yes," Masters said.

Nancy was silent. Then she said, "How did you know?"

"It occurred to me that Larry Connor might have tried to commit suicide after all and that, having tried, he might have had a change of mind and attempted to get help—it's a common reaction among many would-be suicides. I checked with the telephone company and located the operator he had dialed. She remembered putting the call through for him. It was to the Richmond residence, to Dr. Jack Richmond. Connor, of course, knew nothing of the emergency call that had taken Dr. Richmond to the hospital.

"The conclusion was obvious. Since Jack Richmond wasn't home when the operator got the Richmond home for Connor, the phone must have been answered by Richmond's wife. It was Vera Richmond, then, who had talked to Larry Connor, heard what he had done to himself, heard him plead for help. It was obviously an emergency, and she had been a trained nurse; she knew her husband was at the hospital for another emergency and time was important; it was logical to suppose that she responded to Larry Connor's plea for help herself. If so, she was the one in Connor's office, not her husband. She was the one who found Larry dead—or let him die, as we now know—and who manipulated everything afterward, including killing Lila Connor."

Nancy found herself full of tremors, cold and trembling. She hugged her knees to her chest for warmth. But she was still cold.

"I can't believe it," she said. "Vera . . . Vera is the last one I would have suspected."

Masters said, "She's the last one *I* suspected, Mrs. Howell."

"Jack must have known what he would find here. He seemed to—to *accept* it."

"He was afraid of something of the sort. For that matter, so was I. That was why I went looking for him." Masters hesitated. "In a case like that, a husband has the right to be the first to know."

"How understanding of you, Lieutenant."

"I'm sorry," he said.

"Are you?" Nancy set her little jaw and cried, "I don't believe you. You're a—a *scavenger!* Larry and Lila and Vera—all dead. I hope you're satisfied!"

Masters did not protest the injustice of it.

He followed Nancy Howell through the hall and across the kitchen, and he stood in the Richmonds' back door watching her run across the yards in the fierce sunlight. He continued to stand there after she disappeared in her own house. He felt drained, empty, a fat and ugly husk. Masters was not satisfied with many things in his life, and it was long past the time for trying to do something about it, and she smelled so nice, and tomorrow might be better for him than today, but he doubted it.